C000019379

To Barbara.

Astrid Klemz.

Reading in the
Shower

PlaneTree

Reading in the Shower

by

Astrid Klemz

Published 2004
ISBN 1-84294-149-6

Published by PlaneTree

Old Station Offices,
Llanidloes,
Powys SY18 6EB
United Kingdom

Manufactured in the United Kingdom

Dedication: To Elizabeth

CONTENTS

Muddying the Waters.

Pat looked out of the window and chuckled. There, standing on the edge of the pond just as though he was peering into the depths, stood a garden gnome. Somebody must have put it there for a joke; everybody knew how she hated the things.

It looked very lifelike. The red jacket and trousers hung realistically on his squat figure and the outsize boots looked well worn in. She'd give it to the Oxfam shop tomorrow; they'd get a good price for it. Meanwhile she'd got the tea to prepare. Her niece and the children were coming; they'd be here in a few minutes. She'd better put the gnome in the shed before they saw it or she'd never live it down!

She went to pick up the gnome and was surprised when it skipped neatly out of reach.

'Goodness gracious,' she said. 'What on earth are you doing in my garden?'

'I'm a detective, Madam,' he said pompously. 'I'm looking for a missing person.'

Pat felt ashamed for having asked. Though he was less than a foot high the little man's manner made her feel even smaller.

'Do you mind very much going away,' she said shyly. 'I'm expecting visitors and...' she hesitated, not quite knowing how to say that she didn't want her family to think she kept garden gnomes. 'They've got children and they might interrupt your work,' she said lamely.

'Have you cleaned this pond out recently?' The little man demanded.

'Um...no.' Pat didn't like his hectoring tone but didn't like to say so. 'But your missing person wouldn't be hiding in a pond, would he?'

'He might.'

'Would your person be your size or mine?' Pat didn't know the politically correct term for people under one foot high.

'He'd be more my size than yours.'

'Well if I see anyone your size I'll let you know. How do I get in contact with you?'

'Just call my name – I'm Sergeant Brumble – and I'll come.'

Pat heard the sound of a car turning the corner. 'Here they are now. Please hide.'

Sergeant Brumble disappeared. Pat shook her head wonderingly. She'd often told stories about fairies to her nieces and nephews but she'd never really believed in them.

When her guests left Pat searched the garden thoroughly. She even unlocked the shed and pulled out all the tools but all she found were spiders.

She saw Sergeant Brumble on and off over the next few days but he didn't acknowledge her. Pat wasn't pleased; it was her garden after all, and he could at least have said good morning. Once, she tentatively asked him if he'd like some tea but he replied testily that he only drank nectar and he'd had his elevenses thank you.

Then one morning she was woken by the sounds of screaming and growling from the garden. She raised the curtain and looked out, and saw Sergeant Brumble hitting next-door's cat with what appeared to be a little truncheon.

Unwilling to see an animal mistreated she flung open the window and shouted, 'Hey. Stop hitting that cat.'

'Come down and help. It's got the prince,' shouted Brumble breathlessly.

Still too dark to see properly, Pat could just make out something writhing in the cat's mouth, and it was emitting a high pitched trilling scream. Without stopping to put on slippers and dressing gown she raced out into the garden.

'Get hold of it behind the head,' Sergeant Brumble ordered.

Pat grabbed the cat by the scruff. It growled threateningly, but didn't let go of the squealing mouthful.

'Drop that!' ordered the sergeant, giving the cat a sharp whack on the nose with his truncheon.

The cat yelped and dropped its burden, then ran off into its own garden as Brumble bent down to inspect the small green frog trembling at his feet.

'You got me out of bed for a *frog?*' said Pat indignantly.

'His Royal Highness has been turned into a frog,' said Brumble, in tones that suggested that she ought to have known it all along.

'Is it all right?' she asked.

The look Sergeant Brumble gave her would have quelled a politician.

'His Royal Highness is not all right. Though he may only have suffered a few scratches, he still needs to be restored to his proper form.'

The frog croaked crossly.

Sergeant Brumble lost his temper. 'Don't you grumble at me Your Highness. If I had my way you'd be left as you are; it's no more than you deserve. So just keep quiet until this lady's turned you back into a prince again.'

'What do you expect me to do? I don't know how to turn frogs into princes!' exclaimed Pat.

'Kiss it of course. It's got to be kissed by a maiden.'

'Who, me!' Said Pat indignantly.

'Why not. You're a maiden aren't you? I distinctly heard your great nephew referring to you as the maiden aunt.'

Maiden or not there was no way Pat was going to kiss a frog. She'd nothing against them of course, but she was strongly opposed to kissing, or indeed touching in any way at all, the various members of the amphibian family. Frantically, she thought for an excuse.

'I can't. I don't want to marry a prince and have to cope with all that press harassment,' she said with sudden inspiration.

'Oh don't worry, he won't marry you,' Brumble said disparagingly. 'He never marries them,' he added as an afterthought. 'That's why the witch turned him into a frog. She just got to him in time to save her daughter's reputation.'

Pat laughed. The frog croaked angrily.

'Come come, Madam. There's nothing to be afraid of, just pick it up and kiss it.'

That did it. Pat wasn't going to be accused of cowardice by some pompous little man less than a foot high. She bent down and took the frog into her hands. She'd kiss it on the top of its head she thought; that shouldn't be too bad. She always kissed babies on the top of the head where there weren't any unreliable orifices.

She shut her eyes tightly and shuddered as her lips touched something cold and rubbery. Then suddenly, they felt smothered in hair and her hands sagged under the weight of something warm and heavy. She opened her eyes, to find herself clutching a small man, quite handsome if you could ignore his pointy ears. And he was quite, quite naked.

She lowered him to the ground. Brumble ran towards him hastily unbuttoning his tunic.

'Cover yourself Your Highness,' he said, thrusting the garment against the prince's waist and attempting to tie it round him by the sleeves. 'Cover yourself up in front of the lady.'

'Oh don't worry about me,' said Pat. 'I've seen my nephews naked often enough and he's much smaller than they are.'

The prince was incensed.

'Couldn't you have found me a better maiden than some old bat with grey hair and bunions,

Brumble?'

Pat resisted the urge to tread on him. Grey hair and bunions indeed!

'Her Majesty has given me orders to keep you away from young maidens,' retorted the gnome. 'And this lady's just rescued you from an amphibious fate, so the least you can do is to thank her, Your Highness.'

The prince adopted a haughty pose that would have been impressive if he hadn't had Brumble's red tunic tied around his middle. He extended a hand, presumably for Pat to kiss. She ignored it.

Brumble had had enough. 'We ought to return to the palace and let Their Majesties hear the good news Sir,' he said firmly, and giving the tunic a sharp twitch to make sure it covered the prince's rear view properly, he turned him round and propelled him off in the opposite direction.

'Thank you for your assistance Madam,' he called out over his shoulder. 'You'll be suitably rewarded.'

Pat tried to forget Brumble and the Prince though it wasn't easy: there were frogs everywhere that year. She'd never seen so many little ones and could scarcely move for fear of treading on them.

She supposed she must have been rewarded for her efforts, for a Premium Bond that had lain dormant for thirty years finally won £50. Not much reward for kissing a cold rubbery frog then being insulted about her bunions and grey hair afterwards, she thought.

Sergeant Brumble appeared again one afternoon when she was digging the border.

'Yes, what can I do for you Sergeant?' She said crisply.

'I've come to ask you to promise not to kiss any more frogs,' he said.

Pat had had no intention of kissing any more frogs, but she wasn't going to oblige Sergeant Brumble by saying so.

'And why shouldn't I kiss frogs? You seemed quite happy for me to do it last time I saw you.'

'It's the baby frogs, Madam. You may have noticed that there's quite a lot of them about this year.'

'So?'

'It's a bit difficult to explain to a maiden lady.' For once sergeant Brumble seemed uncertain what to say.

Pat sat silently waiting for him to go on.

He gathered himself with an effort. 'When His Highness was living as a frog, it was springtime you understand.'

Pat was indeed beginning to understand, but she

8

wasn't going to let Brumble know. She'd let the pompous little upstart spell it out and suffer the embarrassment.

'And as frogs breed in the Spring, Madam, Their Majesties are concerned that some of the froglings might not be entirely amphibian in their genetic content.'

'You mean he spent his time begetting tadpoles and my garden's full of little princes in disguise?'

'No madam. Little crossbreeds, half frog and half fairy. Their Majesties are concerned at the ethical problems that could arise if this were found to be the case.'

And the scandal too, thought Pat.

'So we just leave them as frogs. Isn't that rather cruel?'

'No Madam. They couldn't be happy if they were changed, for they would be neither one thing nor the other. Better to leave them as they are.'

Pat agreed with him entirely but she didn't say so. This time she'd stick out for decent terms.

'I'll consider your proposal,' she said coldly. 'But I'll expect a better reward than a £50 Premium Bond win. I haven't forgotten the prince's rude remarks about grey hair and bunions.'

'I'll convey your message to Their Majesties,' said Brumble humbly.

Next morning when Pat looked in the mirror she saw that her hair had returned to its original mouse brown. Then she looked down at her feet and saw that her two big toe joints were beautifully straight. Obviously Their Majesties had got the message.

She smiled and went out to buy a lottery ticket.

There's No Such Thing as Luck.

Father O'Malley loved cats. Unfortunately, his sister who kept house for him didn't. They were nasty dangerous things, she said. On the way to her wedding she'd tripped over a black cat and broken an arm and both legs, and by the time she was out of hospital Jack had gone off and married someone else.

Jack moved to another parish but gradually the stories filtered back. First he'd lost his job, then they heard he was drinking heavily and couldn't keep jobs even when they were offered to him. The final disgrace came when too drunk to drive, he'd driven his car into a tree and his wife had been killed. Jack went away to Australia after that and they heard no more about him.

'Maybe that little cat brought you luck after all,' said Father O'Malley to his sister when they

11

received news of the latest tragedy.

'There's no such thing as luck. It's superstitious nonsense and you know it.'

'Well now if God created cats couldn't he have created the black ones lucky?' Father O'Malley's eyes twinkled. He enjoyed teasing his sister.

He had to content himself with making friends with every cat in the parish. He knew all of them by name and always asked after them when his parishioners greeted him outside church on Sundays.

Apart from her dislike of cats his sister was a wonderful woman and Father O'Malley frequently had cause to bless the little cat that'd tripped her up on her wedding day. She ran the house like clockwork. A superb cook, she was famous for her pies and won all the prizes for bakery at the annual show.

It was the pies that started her off on the parish visiting. When one of his parishioners died suddenly leaving a husband and two sons to fend for themselves, Father O'Malley suggested it would be an act of kindness to take them one of her steak and kidney pies.

He hoped she'd like visiting: he felt she didn't get out enough. Still a handsome woman she should be finding a nice husband for herself, but when he'd suggested that she should mix more she didn't seem interested. There was a schoolteacher who'd come to live in the parish and for a while she seemed to like him, but when he inherited his grandmother's cat – a grumbling old thing that bit people – she lost interest.

'I like visiting,' she said on her return from the bereaved family. 'Do you think I could help with it on a permanent basis? I know you're overworked since the curate got his own parish.'

Father O'Malley thought this a splendid idea. Not only would it get her out meeting people it would get her acquainted with some of their pets, and surely having met such lovely animals she'd relent and let him have a cat of his own.

'I'd love you to share the visiting,' he said. 'How shall we divide it? Shall I take the families on the left of the main road and you do the right?'

'No,' she said with a grin. 'You do the houses with cats and I'll do the ones without.'

Father O'Malley sighed. He'd never get his own cat at this rate. Every cat in the district came running up to play with him but it wasn't the same as having his own.

His sister made a marvellous parish visitor – almost as good as a curate they said – but it was in the winter that she really showed her worth. That winter was the worst the town had known for years and lots of old people became ill or slipped down and broke their bones. The priest and his sister were kept fully occupied organising volunteers to do the shopping and take sick people their dinners.

It was the week before Christmas when Father O'Malley fell himself. He'd been working so hard organising emergency services that he'd fallen behind with his usual pastoral work. The Manor had recently been converted into flats for single people and he wanted to welcome the newcomers and invite them to the Christmas celebrations.

When he finally managed to visit it was getting dark, then just before he got to the gate he saw a small black cat sitting on the wall. An adorable little thing, not yet fully grown, it rubbed its head along the coping, purred and waggled its spine, clearly hoping to get his attention. Reaching up to stroke it he failed to see the patch of ice underfoot, slipped, and fell heavily onto the pavement.

A passing motorist took him to surgery.

'It's only a sprain Father,' said the doctor as he bandaged his ankle. 'I'll give you a prescription to get rid of the swelling. You'll not be able to get around on it for a few days but I expect you can say Mass sitting down.'

Father O'Malley was very disappointed. He'd so

much wanted to invite the new residents to join in the festivities. There were to be hot drinks and mince pies in the hall on Christmas Eve and a ramble with the other churches on Boxing Day.

He asked his sister if she'd mind visiting instead. He hadn't wanted to bother her this week as she was in charge of the catering, but there really wasn't much option.

'Yes of course I'll go. Mind you if I see that little cat that tripped you up I might forget that this is the season of goodwill and throw something at it.'

'It didn't trip me up; I slipped on the ice. The cat had nothing to do with it.'

She smiled as she closed the door.

Father O'Malley looked forward to having the house to himself for an hour or two. He'd open the bottle of sherry one of his parishioners had given him then he'd put his feet up and read that new detective novel. Engrossed in his book, he didn't notice that his sister was away longer than usual and it wasn't till he felt the cold draught of the door opening that he realised how late it was.

'Sorry I'm a bit late. I got caught up with something.' She looked happy. 'Can I join you in a drink, I've got good news for you.' She poured herself a glass of sherry, then clinking glasses said. 'Cheers. Would you like to have a cat?'

'I'd love to have a cat, but there's no way you're going to let me.'

She ignored him and went on talking. 'A man's going to get married and his fiancee can't stand cats. Would you like it?'

'Of course I'd like it but don't tell me you're ever going to live with a cat, not even with a glass of sherry inside of you.'

'But *I'm* not going to live with the cat, *you're* going to live with the cat. Jack's back from Australia. He's never touched a drop since the accident and we're going to get married as soon as we can get the banns read. Do you think your ankle will be well enough for you to do my wedding in January?'

Matters Arising

Bill had had a tiring day. He'd visited two different companies at opposite ends of town. The hotel was on a noisy road, so as soon as he'd finished his meal he thought he'd go out for an hour or two's peace and quiet.

He'd spotted a likely looking pub on the drive in and in lieu of anything better to do, decided to go and look for it. The map in the lobby showed that if he took a quick turn around the corner then a short cut across the churchyard he'd soon be there.

It was a fine summer evening and he looked forward to the stroll through the old part of town. The churchyard with its tall trees and the smell of mown grass was appealing and he lingered a while to look at some of the monuments. There was a fine old marble tomb on the edge of the churchyard, and as he walked towards it he saw that it was cracked along the whole of one side and held together with stout wire. He gave a grunt of disgust. Vandals, he thought, even in this quiet little place. What a shame to see so fine a piece of carving destroyed. He turned away and headed for the pub.

He found the pub almost empty with just an elderly man seated at the bar. The man greeted him as soon as he approached the counter and looked pointedly at his empty glass. Bill recognised the type at once and supressed a smile.

'What'll you have then,' he said. 'Same again?'

'Aye, that'll do nicely thanks.'

The landlord shook his head and made a wry gesture.

'Sim, you're a disgrace,' he said. 'I wonder anyone round here still talks to you.'

'They buys me drinks because Oi be a good conversationalist,' the old man said, giving Bill a gap-toothed grin. 'Just you sit there and ask me anything you like about this town and Oi'll tell 'ee.'

After exchanging a few pleasantries with the landlord, Bill turned to the old man and asked him if there'd been many changes in recent years.

'Precious few, since the shoe factory shut down and put two-hundred and odd people out of a job,' he said.

'And the hippies,' said the landlord.

'Aye, they hippies. They come camping here every summer taking drugs and stealing everything they can carry. They'll be back here any time now.'

'I wish the police would move them on,' the landlord interjected. 'They camp in the cemetery and hang about begging. Some of my customers won't come past them and I lose a lot of trade when they're around.'

'Was it the hippies who broke that lovely marble monument in the churchyard?' Bill enquired.

There was an uncomfortable silence in the bar. Bill felt as though he'd said something tactless, though he couldn't see what.

Sim settled himself more firmly on his stool and gripped his glass tightly, assuming the pose of a raconteur.

'It weren't they hippies who broke open that tomb, it were Lillian Larkin.' He paused for dramatic effect.

'And who's Lillian Larkin when she's at home?' Bill knew he was expected to ask the question.

'That tomb's 'er home, 'er last resting place it's supposed to be, but she don't rest; not all the time she don't.'

Bill waited for more. Long experience of buying drinks for elderly persons in pubs had given him a respect for a tale well told, especially when he didn't believe a word of it.

'Lillian Larkin were thirty years old when she married. That were old to be marrying in those days, but she weren't 'andsome. She were downright ugly, but Ephraim Larkin married her all the same for she were a very wealthy woman and 'ee had nothing but a scrubby bit of land to call 'is own. Lillian were an only child and 'er uncles had no issue so when they died there were three farms and an undertakers business all left to Lillian.

'Now Ephraim Larkin was much younger than she and 'ee had a way with the ladies; some said he had too much of his way with the ladies. But no-one else had offered for Lillian so when 'ee asked her she said yes, and they were married on 'er thirtieth birthday.'

Sim took a long drink of his ale, deliberately to add suspense Bill supposed.

'Now on 'er wedding night, Lillian Larkin went up to bed, but she waited and waited for Ephraim and 'ee never came. An when she were tired of waiting, she went downstairs to look for 'im and she found him frolicking on the floor with the milk-maid.'

Sim took another long drink, stringing out the pause till Bill could have shaken him with impatience.

'I reckon she told him off and 'ee couldn't take it. Anyways 'ee took 'er by the throat and 'ee shook 'er till she was strangled. The milk-maid ran out screaming that Ephraim had killed the mistress and pretty soon young Ephraim was arrested for Lillian's murder.'

He slurped the dregs of his beer noisily. With a resigned sigh Bill bought him another, with the resolve that this would be the last.

'Anyways, Ephraim Larkin was 'anged and the whole of 'is and Lillian's property went to a second cousin of 'ers because there was nobody else to inherit it. But this cousin 'ee did right by Lillian all the same, for when 'ee took over the undertakers business 'ee gave her the finest tomb that money could buy. 'Ee sent to London for a man to carve the angels and some say 'ee sent to London for an expert embalmer as well, though others say 'ee just had it done by the local tanner who put 'er in the tank with all they other bits of leather.'

Sim paused again and looked at his glass expectantly. Bill did not rise to the bait this time.

'So who was it wrecked the tomb then?' Bill said, a trifle impatiently.

''Twas Lillian 'erself split that marble panel asunder,' Sim replied raising his free hand in a dramatic gesture. 'On the thirtieth anniversary of 'er death tis said she rose again, all shrunken and looking like leather and flung herself at a young man on the way to 'is wedding. "Come lie with me, me 'andsome," says Lillian. "Thirty years old Oi be and never once lain with a man." And she refused to go lie in 'er grave till the Vicar came after 'er with 'is bell book and candle and prayed 'er back into the ground.'

'Well that's a good story.' Bill laughed then paused to enjoy his own beer. 'It's a pity someone doesn't get the tomb repaired though. That angel panel's quite something; you don't see workmanship like that nowadays. It looks such a mess with all that baling wire around it.'

Sim bent his head and breathed deeply, deliberately spinning out the tension before raising his head again.

'That wire's not there to hold the panel together,' he said dramatically, 'it's there to stop Lillian Larkin getting out, for the thirty years has come round again.'

Bill looked at the landlord, raising his eyebrows.

The man gave a nervous laugh. 'I've heard the story of course, but I'm not from round here originally so I can't say. There's some that believes she gets up every thirty years to look for a lover and some that doesn't, but it's true about the wire. A bunch of farm labourers came over last week with a reel of the stuff and made a good job of tying Lillian down. Nobody could get out of there now, even if that sort of thing were possible.'

'It be possible all right. I've not seen 'er myself; but I know a man who has.'

Bill thought that if Sim's friends drank as much as he did they'd probably seen a lot worse than a few spectres in the churchyard – unless of course, somebody had played a trick; he'd have done it himself in his younger days.

'But if they believed the story, why did they leave it till last week to come and tie her down?' Bill wanted to know.

'Because tonight's the night!' Sim declaimed.

'That's why my pub's so empty,' chipped in the landlord. 'Nobody wants to come near the graveyard tonight. I'll show you the long way round to your hotel if you like.'

'No don't bother, I'm sure I can find it.'

Bill drank up and left. It was a good story; he'd enjoyed listening to it but he'd heard plenty like it. Men who travel for a living hear a lot of stories when characters like Sim want someone else to buy the drinks.

As it happened he didn't go the long way round,

for when he left the pub it was raining and he didn't want to get his suit wet. It was the only suit he had with him and he had another couple of calls to do tomorrow. He'd take the short cut through the churchyard and so what; he wasn't going to be put off by some silly story from an old scrounger who'd made the whole thing up to keep having his glass refilled.

Bill set off at a smart walk along the street then turned into the cemetery, welcoming the shelter from the trees. He wasn't the only person taking a short cut tonight; he could hear light footsteps coming up behind him. Doubtless it was somebody else who didn't believe in ghosts.

Then suddenly he felt a rush of air, and he was seized round the neck by a pair of cold scrawny arms. He tried to twist himself free but the arms were powerful and drew him closer. There was a strong smell of mouldy leather.

I'm afraid that Bill panicked at this point. He didn't believe a word of old Sim's story of course, but when a cold, mouldy smelling object seizes you round the neck in the middle of a churchyard at night, one is entitled to be at least a little nervous.

'Help!' He yelled. 'Somebody help me!' Alas nobody came, and the scrawny arms clutched even tighter. He could have sworn he heard a sibilant whisper, like the air drawn through a set of ancient bellows; 'Come lie with me, me 'andsome.'

That did it. Bill wasn't exactly virtuous, but the thought of lying with a corpse was too much even for a man of his permissive habits. With a wave of revulsion he kicked out and tore himself free, then fell over one of the creature's feet. The smelly leathery thing gave a cry of glee and slapped itself down on top of him. He felt something horribly bony grinding itself against his teeth.

With a desperate howl, Bill drew up his knees, then thrust them hard away from himself. Whatever it was that had attacked him fell backwards onto the path with the sound of a leather holdall stuffed with coathangers. He didn't wait to look, just pulled himself to his feet and ran towards the streetlights on the other side of the wall. He vaulted over and fell on the wet pavement but pulled himself up quickly and ran as though all the devils in hell were after him. He thought they probably were.

Reaching the hotel, he packed his suitcase and checked out. He'd drive home in the dark and find some excuse for cancelling tomorrow's visits in the morning. He wasn't going to stay in this benighted town any longer.

He calmed down as soon as he joined the motorway; that great monument to modern civilisation, leading to everything that was familiar, scientific and profitable; everything the twenty-first century could offer a man. The stream of cars rushing towards him comforted and restored him. Country towns, old pubs and garrulous old drunks didn't belong in the modern world. Someone had played a trick on him, that was all.

Unless of course it was a hippie. They'd been expecting hippies any time around now. They were usually scrawny – too doped to eat properly he imagined – and of course they smelt. He'd simply been mugged by a hippie who wanted money for drugs. He'd heard that you could tell which drug they were on by the smell of it. He'd ask his nephew next time he saw him which drug smelt like mouldy leather. Fourteen-year-olds knew everything about drugs nowadays.

His wife was pleased to see him, she'd even waited up for him, and as he felt her soft arms go around him and smelt the sweet scent of her favourite bubble bath, he knew that his fears of the supernatural had been groundless. A dead woman couldn't get out of her grave and try to make love to him. One had to be alive, warm, with a beating heart, to become a lover. So he told his wife he'd been the victim of an attempted mugging and had decided to come home early. If he told her the story he'd heard in the pub she'd have thought he'd gone mad.

The following Sunday his wife was reading the paper over breakfast and she suddenly laughed aloud.

'Oh Bill, here's such a funny story about that place where you were last week. Some hippies ran into the police station and asked the officer at the desk to arrest them. They said they'd been so stoned they'd had relations with a mummified corpse.'

Bill choked over his coffee cup. His wife didn't notice and carried on reading.

'They begged the officer to lock them up,' she read. 'They asked for a cell with lots of locks on the door and not to let them out again. The sergeant committed them to the cells overnight for their own safety with a view to questioning them properly when they'd sobered up, but next morning they refused to leave and demanded access to a rehabilitation centre. "We may be drug addicts," one of the men said, "but we don't mess with corpses."

Bill's wife chortled and continued to read. 'The four men were charged with drug offences and with malicious damage to a marble vault in the cemetery, though they denied the latter. All were given custodial sentences.

'The body was reinterred in a new grave. Our reporter visiting the scene was told by a resident that the spirit of a woman murdered on her wedding night rises every thirty years to seek a lover. The man telling the tale said, 'Now she's got what she wants Oi reckon she'll stay down there.'

Bill didn't believe a word of it of course, but he made sure he never did business in that little town again.

The Colour Red.

I'd always hated red. Red flowers, red pictures, red shoes; I only had to see the colour and I'd want to scream. My foster parents were very good about it. They never had red things in the house and Mam always kept the meat out of sight till she'd cooked it.

I'd always known I was fostered. I called her Mam because Gareth did, though I called his dad Uncle John. Mam used to laugh about it if people said anything. 'You'd think we were having an irregular relationship, wouldn't you,' she'd say.

The school was very understanding too. I went to nursery class with Gareth when I was about three and the teachers used to pick me up and cuddle me whenever I panicked. I think they must have asked the other parents not to put their children into red clothes for I never saw any at school and I know they never had tomato sauce at dinnertime. Sometimes the other kids tried to tease me about it but Gareth always protected me. He once hit a little boy who tried to put my head inside a red carrier bag.

I must have been about six when some people in our street painted the house door scarlet. We had to walk all the way up the hill and down the other side of the block if we wanted to go out anywhere.

Uncle John got a bit cross then. 'I think it's time she grew out of it,' he said shortly.

'She is growing out of it, aren't you Love,' said Mam, giving me a hug. 'Leave it to nature John. It'll sort itself out in good time.'

I wasn't growing out of it; I'd just learnt to look away whenever I saw something red then go out of the room as soon as possible. If it got too bad though, I couldn't help it and I'd scream. A girl in my class had a nosebleed and I screamed so hard the classroom assistant had to carry me outside and I couldn't come back till they'd cleaned all the mess up.

By the time I was seven I'd become very good at getting away from red and I hadn't had any panic attacks for months so Uncle John took Gareth and me to the zoo. He'd planned it so that we didn't have to see the lions and tigers feeding. I loved seeing all the animals, especially the llamas and the goats that let you pet them. I had to leave the parrot house because some of the birds had red on them and Uncle John said I was a good girl to be so sensible.

Then we went to see the monkeys and as soon as they saw us coming they all bent down and showed us their bottoms, bright red like raw meat. I panicked. I tried looking away but whichever way I turned I could see those horrible animals waggling their crimson behinds at me. I screamed a lot then. Gareth took me by the hand and dragged me out of the door, but there was a bed of bright red geraniums nodding their heads at me and I carried on screaming. I could tell Uncle John was fed up with me because he wore that rigid look on his face but he didn't say anything. Then an old lady came up and said, 'That child's a spoilt brat and you ought to give her a good smacking.'

Uncle John picked me up then and gave me a cuddle, carrying me out to the car park saying things like, 'never mind pet,' and 'it's all right now, I've got you,' until we were in the car and safe again.

They didn't take me anywhere again for a while. There was a nice lady who came to see me at school then arranged for me to come and see her at home.

She had a lovely cat called Sam and she let him sit on my knee. She said he was a British Blue but of course he wasn't blue at all, he was a lovely smoky grey, like the clouds when the sun has just gone in. The lady said I'd have to get used to seeing red because there were so many red things in the world, and didn't I like roses?

I started to shiver when she said that. I hated roses. It wasn't just their colour, roses scratched people and made them bleed. She said you could get a pure white thornless rose that smelt wonderful and wouldn't I like to see one but I said no; I never wanted to see a rose.

She said not to worry. There was no hurry; we could get used to red things bit by bit. She'd introduce me to things that were only a little bit pink at first. The next time I went she showed me a pale pink scarf with green leaves on it and said I had to look at it while I stroked Sam. Then she said she'd like me to touch the scarf when I felt ready. I wasn't worried so I reached out to touch it, only Sam got his paw in first and swatted it out of her hand then jumped down and started to drag it around the floor playing with it. We both had good laugh and she said I was coming along well.

Actually I wasn't. The scarf didn't frighten me because it wasn't that sort of pink. It was a kind of peachy pink like pale orange. I don't mind orange. I like tangerines and carrots and marigolds and marmalade cats. Anyway the lady must have said that I was progressing because Mam said we could all go on holiday to Majorca.

'We haven't had a proper holiday for years,' she said.

Gareth had never been on holiday and neither had I. Mam said I mustn't scream if I saw anything red in Majorca.

'We're going to a foreign land and we have to be polite to the people who live there. If you start to scream they'll think you don't like their country, so if you see anything you don't like just tell Uncle John or me and we'll take you away from it. You're a big girl now; do you think you can manage to do that?'

I wasn't sure, but Gareth said he'd look after me and anyway, I could see that the others really wanted to go so I said I was sure I'd be all right.

I think my foster parents must have told the hotel about my problem because there wasn't anything red in our bedroom; they had even put green apples in the bowl. There was no tomato ketchup on our table, and the head waiter had given us a table where we didn't have to look at what other people were eating. There was a mark on the wall in the lounge and I heard a lady say she wondered why they'd taken down the picture of the Spanish dancer.

I liked Majorca. The little harbours were lovely, with small boats with white sails scudding in and out of them. We went to some big caves where a barge sailed out onto a lake and the people on it played lovely music. There were stalagmites and stalactites down there too. Some of the little kids cried because it was a bit dark in places but I didn't mind; I'm not afraid of the dark. We went to an enormous market where Mam bought a handbag. There was a bit of red there – you know, awnings, bars of soap with pictures of ladies with red dresses on the wrapper – but I just looked away. There was so much else to see.

I cut my foot on a piece of broken glass on the beach. Gareth wasn't with me that time because Mam had given me the money and I'd run back to buy the ice creams. I started to scream then, but a nice German lady poured some water out of a bottle onto my foot to wash the sand away and dried it on a towel. She stuck a plaster over the cut and as soon as I couldn't see the blood anymore I was all right. Mam came up and thanked her. I don't think the German lady knew any English but she must have understood what Mam was saying because they both smiled at each other.

'She's coming on really well,' I heard Mam say to Uncle John when they thought Gareth and I had gone off to play outside. Actually we were sitting on the floor behind the settee playing marbles where they couldn't see us.

'Let's hope she's really growing out of it at last. I'll be frank with you: I can't stand much more of it.'

'I know that, John. Sometimes I can scarcely stand it myself. But we have to stand it. She's our little girl now and we're all she's got.'

There was a nice old couple at the hotel who used to talk to us in the lounge. One evening they said they'd been to a lovely restaurant up in the mountains.

'It's run by such charming young people,' they said. 'They're English and they came here about five years ago. He does the cooking and she's in charge of the dining room. They found this place with a wonderful view over the cliffs and you can watch the waves breaking below you as you eat. And as for the food, it's superb!'

Uncle John said he'd take us there for lunch and combine it with a trip to the northern part of the island. We drove along a twisty road that crept around cliffs topped with dark green pine trees, the sun glistening on the bright blue sea below us. We stopped at a place where a man was making glass jugs by blowing into a great orange bubble of glass through a long black tube. When he saw Gareth and me he stopped blowing bubbles and started making little glass animals. He made a green rabbit for me and a blue and white sausage dog for Gareth. There was a black and white cat walking about between the glassblowers' legs. The white bits were all smudged and sooty. It came out when it saw us and we stroked it.

We went further and further up the mountains till we came to the restaurant, set high on a headland. Far below us the sea was dark blue, almost navy, with white frills of foam where the rocks were sticking up through it.

'Oh how lovely,' Mam said as we parked in the courtyard.

We looked over the wall to where the cliff showed all rough and rugged. Uncle John pointed to a dark shadowed cleft below a jutting outcrop.

'I'm sure that's a cave,' he said.

We went into the restaurant. I can't remember very much about it except that the lady was very pretty and everybody was nice to Gareth and me.

I could hear people talking behind us. 'The chef always comes out to greet the visitors,' somebody said.

I turned and saw a man dressed all in white with a funny tall hat talking to some people at the other end of the room. He walked slowly past all the tables, shaking hands with the guests and there was lots of chatting and laughter.

Then he came to our table; and I screamed.

I screamed and I screamed. I couldn't stop screaming. Uncle John started to say something, then didn't. I could see he was cross.

Mam picked me up and carried me out of the door to the car park. She was talking to me but I couldn't take in what she was saying. All I knew was that I'd got to get away and hide, but I couldn't because Mam was holding me so tightly.

I could hear people talking around me, then Uncle John came out and said that the lady had sent for a doctor. Mam turned to listen to what Uncle John was saying and I felt her grip slacken, so I wriggled out of her arms and ran for the cliff. I had to find the cave, then I'd wriggle into the tightest little corner and hide.

I ran to the wall and scrambled over the edge. Uncle John grabbed me by the arm and pulled. It hurt, so I yelled, but I'd screamed so much anyway that I don't think he noticed. He dragged me back over the wall; grazing my knee and making it bleed.

I panicked properly then and fell down on the ground, twisting in every direction trying to find something to crawl under.

He crouched down beside me and held me very tightly. After a while someone come and I felt a prick on the arm. I couldn't scream any more; I felt dizzy and I kept being sick.

'Take her back to the hotel and put her to bed; she'll sleep the rest of the day,' said a voice with a Spanish accent. 'Give her one of these tablets if she panics again.'

Uncle John bundled me into the car and I sat on the back seat cuddled up between Man and Gareth. I wanted to go to sleep but I knew I mustn't. I had to tell them to hide; to lie absolutely still and hold their breath so that they didn't make even the tiniest sound.

'What was it, Pet?' Mam turned my head towards her. 'Just tell me what it was and I'll make sure it can't hurt you.'

I couldn't reply. There are some things even a mother can't protect you from. Now he knew where I was he'd come for me; and Mam and Gareth; maybe even Uncle John.

'Tell me all about it, Love,' she said again.

'That was him,'

I said. 'That man with the white clothes on.'

'The chef? What about him?'

'He'll come after us with his big cleaver.'

'Of course he won't,' Uncle John said crossly. 'All chefs have cleavers; they need them for cutting up the food.'

I whimpered and clung harder to Mam.

She held me close. 'You're safe with us, Darling. Nobody can hurt you now.'

'Yes he can. He'll cut us all into little pieces like he did before. The man in the white hat's my Daddy.'

The Skeleton in the Cupboard.

Grandad did trompe l'oeil. You know; those paintings where you think there's a solid object like a statue or a vase of flowers in an alcove, but when you get close up you see it's just a painting done on a flat wall. He pronounced it 'tromple oil' and it all started when he saw a programme about it on the television.

He'd been wanting to do something with the cemetery wall for a long time and when he saw what could be done with a few pots of paint he got a book from the library and had a go. His first efforts weren't too good but he soon got the hang of it, and before long the graveyard wall sprouted urn-filled niches, scrolls and pious looking angels. His finest moment came when somebody complained to the council about wasting money on marble statues and from then on there was no stopping him.

Grandma was in two minds about 'his trompling' as she called it. She was glad he had something to do with his retirement coming on but she wasn't pleased to find a spider glaring up at her when she'd drained the mug of tea Grandad gave her. She was even crosser when he painted a disembowelled mouse on the pantry floor. She hit the cat and it wouldn't speak to her for days. She got used to it all after a while – she always did get used to Grandad's peculiarities – and eventually she became very proud of his achievements.

There was always something fresh to admire at Grandad's place. The hall had originally been dark and poky, but Grandad painted a French window with trees outside on the end wall, and when he switched the lights on you'd really think you were about to step into the garden. Before long the whole place began to look like a stately home. All the ceilings had cornices, and the plain wooden doors were turned into richly panelled porticoes. There were marble statues in niches all the way up the staircase and a cloud-filled skylight hovered above the landing.

But it was the bathroom that really impressed visitors. There were mermaids reaching out to welcome you into the marble pool, great lumps of coral that made you watch out where you put your foot and when you'd finally decided that it was safe to sit down, fishes swimming all round you as you wallowed.

Grandma said the mermaids were rude so Grandad had to go back and paint bras on them.

They had a house next to the cemetery where Grandad used to work. It actually went with the job of gardener and gravedigger, but the man who took over when Grandad retired didn't want the house; he said it made his wife nervous. Grandma didn't mind living near the graveyard; she'd got used to it by now.

Grandad loved it. Even after his retirement he'd walk around putting flowers from his garden on the graves of those who had no one left to care for them. He called it 'paying his respects to the inhabitants'. He'd met quite a number of them in his time and not just recent ones. Old graves weren't recorded, he told us, and he frequently came across their incumbents while digging a new hole. He always treated the skeletons with respect; lifting them tenderly and putting them into a neat plot he'd dug ready for them. He'd given each one a proper name, and he'd turned an old railway sleeper into a lovely marble headstone with all their names carved on it. He said it was to make it up to them for being disturbed and he was sure they'd appreciate it.

Well as I've said, Grandad became very good at his trompling, and then somebody from the local paper came round and published an article on him. Not long after that a man from the Sunday supplements arrived and there was our Grandad in full colour with his mermaids and marble statues smiling out from the centre page spread of a major national newspaper. The proprietor (who was American) must have syndicated the article over there, for the next thing we knew Grandad had been invited to go to the United States to give a lecture at an art symposium.

Grandma got him a new suit and herself a new dress and hat and we gave him an American-English dictionary, just so's he didn't go around calling the cats pussy and referring to erasers as rubbers and shocking the natives. Then we took him to the airport and saw him off. We promised to keep an eye on the house and water the plants and feed the cat.

We watered a few two-dimensional plants and stroked a few false cats before we realised that the naughty old so-and-so had taken the opportunity to play a few more tricks on us. 'Help yourselves to tea and coffee when you come round,' he'd said, but we had to plough through a lot of forgeries before we found the real tins hidden in the back of the pantry. And we all got caught out when we used the loo, flushing it again and again before we realised that the thing in the pan was only another piece of tromp. Each one who got caught didn't tell the others, so that poor old loo got flushed to distraction before we'd done with it.

We'd just been home about an hour after feeding the cat one evening when a policeman came round.

'Your grandad's been burgled,' he said with a laugh.

We didn't think it was funny and said so.

'Oh there's been no harm done,' he said, still chuckling. 'It was old Mikey Molesworth who did it. He'd heard your grandad was away in America, so he thought he'd be in for an easy ride. He got inside easily enough – those door locks wouldn't keep a child out – but when he got in he got the fright of his life. He says he broke into this cupboard and found a skeleton grinning at him. He ran out screaming, straight into the arms of WPC Bouncer on her way back from Kung Fu practise.

The policeman chortled again. 'We saw your grandad's artwork, it would have taken me in if I hadn't read about him in the newspaper. I particularly liked the mermaids. Pity about the old-fashioned bras though; they looked just like my Gran's underwear. Old Mikey Molesworth wouldn't have known about trompe l'oeil: he can't read. He thinks the skeleton in the cupboard's a real one and he swears he's going straight from now on.

'Better go round now and make sure everything's all right,' the policeman continued. 'You'll need to get a new lock for the door tomorrow; we've put a temporary plank and a padlock on it for now.'

We went. Apart from the broken front door lock there wasn't much damage and nothing seemed to be missing. Grandad didn't have anything worth pinching apart from his pension and he'd have had to take that with him for spending money.

We'd never looked in the cupboard under the stairs before. We just assumed it was where Grandma kept the cleaning things. We were quite looking forward to meeting the skeleton; it was bound to be realistic. Grandad had after all, been intimately acquainted with a number of them.

He'd enjoy the story when he got back no doubt, but he'd be annoyed when he saw the damage done to the cupboard door. The thief had taken the poker to what he thought was an antique brass lock. It had been a particularly impressive piece of Grandad's handiwork and none of us had realised it wasn't the real thing until now. The door didn't have a real lock so Mikey Molesworth needn't have battered it to bits like that.

'Serves him right for damaging a work of art,' I said.

There wasn't any skeleton. There was nothing at all in that cupboard except cleaning things, the ironing board and the clothes-horse. We assumed at first that there must have been a painted panel that had fallen down somewhere, or perhaps a roller blind that had sprung up, but though we looked everywhere, we couldn't find anything at all that could have been mistaken for a skeleton. Then we thought that maybe the police had taken it for evidence but when we rang them they said no, there'd been no need.

'Mikey Molesworth made a full confession – glad to get it off his chest in fact – and I can't say that I blamed him. I'd have been taken in myself if I hadn't known. WPC Bouncer says she could have sworn it winked at her. We had a good laugh, then shut the door and left.'

Grandad came home full of his American adventures, which he regaled us with on the way back from the airport and it was some time before we could get a word in edgeways to tell him about the burglary.

'It was a good idea of yours to tromple a skeleton in a cupboard, but the funny thing is, we can't find it anywhere.'

Grandma looked resignedly at Grandad. 'I told you not to,' she said.

'Well it's a good job I did, or we'd have been burgled good and proper.'

'What did you tell him not to do Gran?' I asked.

'Told him not to let it keep an eye on the house for us of course. It's not decent; the dead's supposed to be at rest. It was always trying to do him favours for giving it a proper gravestone. "Why don't you go and have a nice lie down," I'd say to it when it came around. "What's the point of my husband making you a nice grave if you don't lie in it." And give it its due, it always went away when I told it to.

'Look,' she continued. 'Here's a petrol station selling flowers. Hop out and buy it a bunch, then as soon as we get home you can go and put them on its grave and tell it to stay down there for good. I'm not having it rattling around my house. Now that it's taken to winking at young girls goodness knows what it'll be trying to do next.'

Grandad did as he was told, but he got his own back. He painted a skeleton on a spare bedsheet and now Grandma never knows whether it's just a bit of Grandad's trompling or old rattle bones trying to get into bed with her. These days she always makes Grandad get into bed first.

The Nature of the Beast.

I usually stood behind Polly in the fitness class. She always knew what to do and if I forgot my routine I could catch up by watching her. With her short black curls and lithe body she looked just like an elf; skipping her way through the exercises with a little smile on her face.

She said she used to be a dancer and I could well believe it. I wondered why she'd given it up but she said it was because her husband didn't like her being on stage every night and getting home so late.

Being right behind her I noticed at once when she came to class with a bandage on her arm. She moved a little stiffly too, and I wondered if she'd had a fall. As the class progressed blood began to seep through the bandage and I asked her if she was all right; but she said it was nothing.

At the end of class I offered her a lift home. She

hesitated at first, but her arm began to bleed again when she put her sweater on, so she said; 'Yes, all right if it isn't too much bother.'

She lived at the other end of town from me but I didn't tell her. I didn't want to embarrass her. She looked so pale and strained I didn't want her fainting on the way home. She got stiffly into the car, trying vainly to stop the bleeding with an inadequate handkerchief.

'Here, why don't you let me drop you off at casualty,' I said. 'I think you ought to get that arm looked at.'

'No, it's nothing. I'll go and see the doctor if it's still causing trouble in the morning,'

'How did you do it?' I asked.

'The dog bit me.'

'Bit you? You ought to get something done about it if it attacks people.'

'He doesn't usually. He's normally very good. I think I must have trodden on his tail...I wasn't looking where I was going.'

'What sort of dog is it.'

'He's a Doberman.'

'Gosh, you can't have a dog that size biting you whenever it feels like it. Look, you must get some advice. Go and see the vet; maybe he can recommend an animal behaviourist or something.'

'I can't do that; it's my husband's dog. He'd never permit anyone else to interfere with it.'

'Is he very fond of the dog?'

'Oh yes; he adores it, and I do too. This is my road. If you drop me here I'll be all right; it's very hard to turn around when everybody's parked outside. Thanks very much for the lift.'

Polly seemed recovered by class the next week. Her arm was still bandaged but she was moving normally again. She avoided my eye so I didn't speak to her. I assumed she didn't want to discuss the dog. She'd probably chickened out of speaking to the vet and was afraid I'd ask her about it.

That was the last week of term, so I didn't see Polly for a few weeks. Then I saw her in the market the Saturday before the new term began and barely recognised her. Her face was pale and puffy, she had a black eye, one of her cheeks was scraped raw and the black curls were tangled and matted.

'Why Polly, what on earth has happened? You look terrible.'

She forced a smile. 'I'm all right really. It's just the dog. The hot weather's been upsetting him and he went for me again.'

'He bit you on the *face*?'

'Oh no, not on the face. He leapt at me and I collided with the corner of the cupboard, that's all.'

'Have you had it seen to?'

'No, I'm getting over it now. It happened a couple of days ago.'

'And the dog?'

'Oh *he's* all right.'

'You didn't consult the vet?'

She shook her head and looked as though she'd like to walk on, but was too polite to snub me. I wasn't going to be put off. The dog might kill her next time. I'd heard of things like that happening.

'How about a cup of coffee? They do nice pastries in the Honeypot.'

I gestured towards the café and Polly followed. She chose a seat in a quiet corner where she could sit unobserved. We sat in silence for a while. I knew what I had to say but I felt embarrassed and Polly clearly didn't want to discuss it.

Polly was half turned away from me so it was a while before I noticed that she was crying; slow silent tears that ran down her ravaged face to drop unchecked onto her lap.

'Here,' I said reaching for a handful of paper serviettes. 'Have a clean hanky.'

She tried to smile and said a muffled thank you.

'You know what you've got to do, don't you,' I said.

'Oh yes. I know what I have to do. The problem

is I love him so.' She was crying in real earnest now.

'How can you love him when he attacks you every time he feels like it? He's dangerous.'

'He's only done it a few times. Usually he's lovely. He can be ever so affectionate.'

'A few times; how many exactly?'

'Four or five; six maybe, but he hadn't done it for a while so I thought he'd got over it.'

'He hasn't got over it. You must go and see the vet. He might be able to sedate him or suggest a trainer who can help you.'

'Maybe I'll do that,' she said. She blew her nose hard. 'I've got to go now; thanks for listening.'

'Will you be at the class next week?'

Oh I hope so; I do so enjoy it. It's the only thing I have now that I've given up my dancing.' She gave me a watery smile.

Polly wasn't at class the next week. We were all surprised for we knew how keen she was. We were planning to put on our usual display at the end of term and Polly was going to be the leader. I felt uneasy. Had the dog bitten her again? Maybe I should look in on her afterwards.

I approached Polly's part of town with foreboding and had visions of her lying injured on the floor. I parked by the telephone kiosk and walked along the street looking for somebody to ask. A man was clipping his hedge.

'Do you know where Polly lives, please? She has short dark curly hair and she's got a Doberman.'

'There's a Polly lives over there,' he said, pointing to a house half-hidden behind a high wall. 'She's certainly dark haired and curly, but I didn't realise she had a dog.'

I approached the house feeling a little silly. What was I supposed to do, go up to the door and knock saying, 'I've come to see if Polly's all right?' She'd probably think I was just being nosy. I almost turned back.

But I didn't. I couldn't forget that ravaged face. I walked up to the gate in the wall and pushed. The front door lay ahead of me, down a long overgrown drive. I almost chickened out again when I tried to think of what I was going to say and had half turned to go back when I heard a woman's scream.

She screamed again, then burst into hysterical sobbing. 'No, oh no! Get away from me you animal. Get off. Let me go!'

I stopped, momentarily stunned, then ran as fast as I could for the telephone box to dial 999. The operator had to tell me to control myself; to breathe deeply, then tell her exactly what the problem was.

'Police please, and ambulance as well. There's a

woman being savaged by a dog. Please help me. I daren't go into the house. Oh please, please send somebody.'

'Can you stand outside the house to direct the vehicles to the right place?'

'Yes,' I whispered.

I walked back to the house and stayed outside the wall for what seemed hours but was probably only a few minutes. Then a police van screamed around the corner. I pointed to the house and three men wearing protective clothing ran up the drive.

'Stay out of the way,' one of them shouted at me. 'Do you live round here?'

Dumbly I shook my head.

'Then go into the phone box and stay there till we tell you to come out. The dog might rush out when we go in.'

I couldn't see what was happening behind the wall, but it sounded as though they were breaking the door down. There was a lot of banging and shouting, then a splintering crash. An ambulance drew up. The paramedics ran out and rushed through the gate carrying a folded stretcher. 'Oh please, please may Polly be all right,' I breathed.

They seemed to be in the house a long time, before they came out carrying a closely wrapped form. I couldn't see any movement. Was Polly still alive?

One of the police waved to me. 'It's all right. You can come out now,' he said.

'Where's the dog, have you managed to restrain it?'

'There was no dog.' He looked at me oddly. 'No dog, no dog dish, no dog bed; there never was a dog in that house. What made you think she had a dog?'

'She came to class all bandaged up and said the dog had bitten her, then another time she said it had gone for her and knocked her down.'

Two other policemen came out of the house struggling with a man in handcuffs. They pushed him roughly into the van.

'There's your dog,' he said, pointing to the prisoner. 'If that lady lives, he'll get done for GBH. If she doesn't, we'll see to it that her husband gets charged with murder.'

One of Our Appendages is Missing.

Mike woke up in bed in his Aunt Betty's guestroom to find he had a toe missing. I must be dreaming, he thought as he turned over to go to sleep again. He woke a short while later and the toe still wasn't there. He knew he wasn't dreaming this time. Henry was mewing and scratching at the bedroom door demanding to come in for his morning ritual. Nobody could have slept through one of Henry's morning fanfares.

He got up to let Henry in, giving his left foot a thorough scrutiny as he did so. There were definitely only four toes on it. There was no pain, no wound, no scar, no obvious gap in the neat rank of usual appendages, but Mike knew he'd always had five toes on that particular foot and now he only had four. What could have happened to it?

Henry didn't seem to notice anything wrong as he rubbed his head around Mike's feet and ankles. He followed Mike back into bed and snuggled up beside him. Maybe his eyes hadn't woken up yet, Mike decided. Surely he'd see five toes again if he looked properly when he got up to dress?

Henry wasn't his usual self that morning either. Normally he'd cuddle up for a while, then play around the bed a little, sneaking up behind the hillocks preparing to jump out at anything he imagined might move. Then he'd spring up onto the windowsill and make threatening gestures at the birds; you know, those silent, jaw-quivering, teeth-rattling faces a cat makes when it sees a bird but can't get at it because of the glass. That particular morning however, Henry wasn't interested in birds at all, even though they flew twittering all over the garden absolutely demanding to be noticed.

Mike looked for his missing toe again when he got up and he still couldn't find it, but he hadn't time to think about it much because Aunt Betty was calling him to breakfast. She was having some friends in to tea that afternoon and wanted him to run her to the shops for supplies so that she could get the preparations done well before they arrived.

Aunt Betty didn't like being alone, so when Uncle Joe was abroad on business she usually invited someone to stay and often invited all her friends round for tea as well. One of the ladies who came to tea that afternoon seemed to be looking at Mike most oddly. Surely she couldn't have known about the toe? Maybe he had something else missing – an ear or an eyebrow perhaps? A quick check in the hall mirror showed him that there was nothing wrong with his appearance. Then he realised the lady wasn't looking at him at all. She had a false eye and couldn't focus properly. He was sure that this particular lady hadn't had a false eye last time he'd seen her; he'd had cause to remember her particularly piercing stare when he'd contemplated helping himself to the last of the cakes.

There was an oldish man there too whose eyes didn't quite seem to move together. Did he have a false eye too? And goodness! Wasn't that another man with only one ear, and a lady with a thumb missing? Had there been some sort of massive local accident that had involved a lot of people; a supermarket collapsing or a gas explosion perhaps? Mike asked Aunt Betty afterwards but she said she couldn't remember any and no, she hadn't realised that so many people had bits missing.

Mike gradually got used to the idea of having only nine toes. He began to think that perhaps he'd never had a full set of toes on both feet. After all, he'd never actually counted them. Have you?

Perhaps he'd just *assumed* he had a full set because everybody always talked as though people had ten toes. Pictures of bare feet always showed ten toes, and he'd just accepted the idea without thinking. One of his schoolteachers always used to say, 'Never take anything anyone else says as true; go and find out for yourself.' Mike had always thought this a good adage, but he'd never thought of applying it to something as mundane as counting toes.

Maybe everybody else had always known he had a toe missing but had been too polite to tell him? Nowadays people were brought up not to mention deformities; it was politically incorrect. Perhaps he'd just gone through life thinking he was normal and never been told otherwise.

Or maybe having ten toes wasn't really normal at all, just average. He remembered his maths teacher explaining that average didn't mean the same as normal. The average sized boy, he said, wasn't the only normal boy in the class. He was just the boy whose height was in the middle of the range. Perhaps some people had nine toes and other people had eleven. He went to the swimming pool to make a toe count, but most of the swimmers went past too fast for him to see. He *thought* they all had ten toes, but he couldn't have sworn to it.

He didn't go to his aunt's again for some months and when he made his next visit it was summer and lots of people in the village were wearing sandals. He was surprised to see so many other people with fewer than ten toes. Perhaps having fewer toes than average was hereditary. Yes, that must be the answer; all the villagers were related. Consanguinity was said to be rife in these out-of-the way places. His aunt had been born there so of course he must be related too, and that's why he'd never had the full complement of toes.

Then he remembered that he wasn't related to Aunt Betty at all; it was Uncle Joe that was his father's brother. And surely if selective toelessness was hereditary it would be the same toe that was missing in each case? In his aunt's village it wasn't. Sometimes it was the big toe that was missing and sometimes it was one of the others. He gazed and gazed at people's feet whenever he went into the village but it was rarely that he saw two people in succession that had a toe missing from the same place. Curiouser and curiouser.

Uncle Joe was home this time Mike visited. He'd had a bad accident abroad, walked with a stick and was taking a sabbatical until he'd recovered. Mike hadn't seen his uncle for some time and was therefore surprised to see that he had become quite bald. When he'd last seen his uncle he'd had a shock of thick brown hair with a grey streak in the front; now he didn't even have a frill of bristles around his ears.

Mike hadn't realised that people could lose all their hair in just eighteen months. Unless of course it was the shock of the accident that caused him to lose it. He'd read about shock making people's hair go white overnight, so perhaps a sufficiently bad shock could cause it to fall out altogether. But of course he couldn't ask. It might embarrass his uncle.

The second day of his stay Aunt Betty had a job for him. 'Would you go down to the cellar and set a few traps please?' she asked. 'There's been a lot of scuffling down there recently. I'm sure we've got mice. Joe can't go down the steps with his bad leg and you know I can't face dealing with mice.'

Mike did know. He'd often had to rescue a half-fainting Aunt Betty from one of Henry's victims.

'What about Henry?' He gave the cat a pat. 'Can't you take him down the steps and just let him hunt to his heart's content?'

His aunt shook her head. 'Henry seems to have quite gone off mousing these days. He hasn't brought anything in for weeks. It's as though he's lost all his hunting instincts. He just doesn't want to kill anything anymore.'

Mike thought this was a distinct improvement. Though fond of cats in general, he'd always thought he'd like them even more if they weren't so cruel. Henry without his sadism would be a lot nicer to have around, even if it did mean somebody else having to go and mess around with mousetraps.

Aunt Betty handed him the traps and some bits of bacon rind for bait. He opened the cellar door and switched on the light.

There was a man in the cellar! A very strange looking man, his face was a mass of folds and ridges that seemed to have been assembled from a collection of small pink sausages. His nose looked just like somebody's big toe set on the wrong way round and his eyes didn't quite match. His lips were cylindrical and wrinkled and rolled up at the front just as though they had been made out of...well... toes! The only thing normal about the man was his hair. He had a thick shock of brown hair with a streak of grey at the front, just like the hair Uncle Joe used to have before his accident.

The man stood there staring at Mike, blinking in the light. Then his lips drew back in a silent snarl, his jaw trembled and his teeth clattered like soundless castanets, just as Henry used to do before he lost his aggression. Mike had just time enough to see the man collect his rear quarters under him before he pounced....

The Homecoming.

Alice sat on the seat trying valiantly to remain upright. If only she didn't feel so weak. She mustn't let herself faint in a public place, especially in front of the stern-looking gentleman opposite. He'd be bound to disapprove of a woman in her situation.

She ought to be glad she was returning to her home town where she knew everyone and had many friends, but as the train passed through the familiar countryside she could think only of her father's cruel rejection.

She'd ached with homesickness these last few weeks, longing for her warm pretty bedroom with its gay curtains and rugs, and her paintings books and childhood toys ranged neatly along the shelves. Now, she'd never be allowed in the house again.

'I'm sending you home,' the doctor had said as he put his stethoscope away. 'You don't belong here.

Go home to your mother.'

'I have no mother. She died when I was little', Alice replied.

'Can you not go to your father? Or a married sister, or an aunt?'

Dumbly, she shook her head. 'I have no father.'

Tears filled her eyes as she remembered the harsh tones of his letter. "You have brought disgrace upon the family...never want to see you again...your sister's fiancee has with difficulty been persuaded to honour his obligations...."

Her aunt had enclosed a note, short but sharp with disapproval. "I am glad my poor dear sister did not live to see this day."

The doctor had been kind, but firm. 'I simply do not believe that a young lady of your breeding has nowhere to go. Perhaps if you wrote asking for forgiveness, one of your relatives might take you in.'

She shook her head. She would never ask for forgiveness; she was not ashamed of what she'd done.

'You cannot look after yourself and I do not think that you would like to be in the sort of establishment meant for women who have no means of support.'

Alice flushed angrily. She was not destitute. Her

mother had left her a small sum of money and as soon as she'd recovered she planned to enrol on one of the courses that trained women to use typewriting machines.

'I have a little money and perhaps my old nanny would let me come and stay for a while.'

'Is she capable?'

'Oh yes. She is not so very old, and she lives in a most comfortable cottage.'

The doctor had telegraphed Nanny who had replied promising to come and meet the next train.

Too weak to think properly, Alice had forgotten that Nanny received her pension from the family and lived rent-free in a cottage on her father's estate. Now speeding homewards, she realised that harbouring Alice against her father's wishes could bring down retribution upon the old woman and she worried lest her thoughtlessness would deprive Nanny of her home and income.

Nanny had always kept in touch. She had never chided her for going away but only said how much she missed Alice and wanted to see her again. It was Nanny who had told her about her sister's wedding and how lovely the bride looked, and how the naughty little page boy had tied the bridesmaid's sash to the pew end so that when the procession moved off she couldn't follow the bride out of the church door. Alice smiled at the recollection; she knew the little lad and his mischievous ways. Then she felt sad again as she remembered how they'd always planned that she would be her sister's bridesmaid. She'd written to congratulate the bride but had received no reply.

Nanny had said she thought Alice's father must have been missing her, for he always looked sad since she'd gone away. She'd hinted that he might be forgiving if Alice made the first step towards making up, but Alice could not forget the harsh tones of his letter. He'd written again, but unable to bear any more of his recriminations, she'd thrown his letters in the fire unopened.

She hoped Nanny would not plague her to apologise to her father. He was naturally austere in manner and when angry could be terrifyingly distant. Nanny had always told her how much he'd loved her mother and as she grew older and understood more Alice realised that her arrival had heralded her mother's death. She'd always admired the stern dignified man, but from a distance, leaving it to her sister to provide the companionship and affection he didn't seem to need from her.

The train lurched over the points and Alice swayed forward, weakness overcoming her. She hauled herself upright and closed her eyes. The train was slowing now.

'May I assist you madam?' It was the gentleman sitting opposite.

'Perhaps you would care for some tea,' he continued. 'We are coming into a station and I intend to call for some refreshments.'

Alice opened her eyes and tried to smile as she thanked him. Yes, she would like some tea, she said, but she refused his offer of sandwiches saying she was not hungry. Her bruised mouth and broken teeth made eating difficult. She could not risk drooling and dropping food in front of a stranger.

The tea refreshed her. She hadn't realised she was so thirsty. She sat upright and smiled at the gentleman.

'Will there be anyone to meet you at your destination?' he said.

'Oh yes, my old Nanny will be there.'

Then having satisfied himself that Alice was not going to faint on the platform and be any further liability, the gentleman retreated into silence again behind his newspaper.

As the train slowed down in readiness for Alice's station, the gentleman looked up again and asked if he might carry her travelling bag onto the platform for her. She thanked him and said that would be very kind. She felt near to tears at the thought that a total stranger was offering her kindness when her own kith and kin had abandoned her.

She could see her father's factory now, the smoking chimneys giving her a further pang of homesickness. The hooter sounded signalling the end of shift. Suddenly the gates opened and a rush of factory girls spilled out into the lane, pulling their coats on, their piece bags banging against them as they ran.

Why were they running so fast? They were making straight for the station. Could they have booked an evening excursion? Surely not at this time of year. The train had stopped and she could see them clearly now, rushing through the gates onto the platform. One of the girls — surely that must be Millie with the long fair hair — was marshalling them into line as though waiting to greet the Mayor or some other important personage.

She felt a stab of fear. She'd hoped to arrive quietly and slip away with Nanny without attracting the attention of anyone who might tell her father he'd seen her. Now this official party had arrived to spoil her chances, and everybody else in town seemed to be converging upon the platform to join them.

The gentleman opened the carriage door for her and as he assisted her down the steps, she could hear the sound of a coach being driven into the station yard. She glanced up and gave a cry of alarm. It was her father's coach; those beautiful bays were unmistakable. She had no chance of avoiding him now.

She could see her father getting out of the coach, scanning the platform as though looking for somebody, and horror of horrors, there was Nanny beside him. Had Nanny, frightened she would lose her cottage and pension, turned traitor and betrayed Alice's homecoming?

The gentleman had returned to the carriage now and she stood alone, swaying weakly on the platform. Suddenly one of the factory girls shouted, 'there she is!' Then they all started cheering and waving. Alice looked around for the celebrity. If the person they were waiting for alighted from the other end of the train maybe she could slip away unobserved and go to the hotel. With luck she'd get away tomorrow and find somewhere to stay out of reach of her father's anger.

Alas there was no escape; her father had seen her. He was striding swiftly towards her, his astrakhan overcoat flapping about his legs and his top hat askew. She closed her eyes. She felt his hands grasp her shoulders. She flinched, awaiting the inevitable angry exchange.

It didn't happen.

Instead he embraced her. 'My darling daughter. Why didn't you answer my letters? I wrote to say I understood but you never replied. Then when I knew what they were doing to you in that prison, I went to ask my MP to get you released, but he said that if a bunch of silly women wanted to starve themselves to death, the sooner they succeeded the better.'

He turned her round to face the cheering crowd.

'Here is our brave suffragette,' he called, as the crowd cheered.

Then he put his arms around her and held her close.

'Welcome home.'

The Medium and the Message.

Madame Mocassa had Mediums' Block. She just couldn't get her act together. She couldn't summon up a spirit, though this wasn't surprising for she'd never summoned up a spirit in her life. She didn't believe in them: she knew they didn't exist. Her mother had told her so.

'All you need is a good act and a knowledge of human nature,' she'd said when she was inducting Mo into the family business. 'Gadgetry's useful but if you've got what it takes you can do your performance on an open beach. Your grandmother once did it for a bet.'

Madame Mocassa couldn't remember a time when she wasn't a medium. Her mother had started her off early. As soon as she'd got Mo into nursery school she'd shown her how to convince the other little girls that she could see the fairies and by the

73

time she moved up to infants, she had the whole school – including the headmistress – seeing fairies too.

At sixteen, she'd been sent to help Auntie Sue (Madame Sukarti) with her seances. She had to pretend to be a member of the audience and get up and shout things like 'That's him', or 'I do so miss you Granny', when appropriate. She also had to get the other clients chatting. People were drawn to the solemn, apparently grieving young girl and she soon had them telling her all about themselves.

'Get to know as much about them as you can and then you're half way there,' her mother had advised. The confidences went straight to Auntie Sue of course.

Mo's father was an engineer. He'd first met her mam when he came to one of her seances. He didn't believe in spiritualism but as he couldn't work out how she did it he'd asked her out, and before he knew where he was he was asking her to marry him. She wouldn't tell him anything until after the honeymoon (in case he felt tempted to set up in business for himself) but as soon as he was properly in the family she had him inventing better scenery and props.

Mo's grandma never approved of Mo's dad. She said a medium didn't need all those tricks and frippery. She never used anything herself, other than a darkened room and a few candles. Mo's mam said Gran *was* good, one of the best in fact, but it did annoy her when Gran would insist that her spirits were real. 'If you believe that you'll believe anything,' she said.

When Mo was twenty-one, her mam and dad set her up in business as Madame Mocassa. They bought her a nice big Victorian house with a cellar deep enough to take a trapdoor and a living room wide enough for a false wall or two. Dad made some lovely gadgets. There was a steam machine that sent up clouds of mist, and a back projection screen that looked like a solid wall. He put recorders in shielded alcoves and set them to make the voices sound distant. Best of all was the drum pedal he'd taken from a second-hand one-man band. It allowed Mo to rap the table while her hands were in full view of the audience.

Madame Mocassa was an instant success. Her youth as well as her skill, and her genuine sympathy with the bereaved made her the most popular medium in London. By the time she was twenty-five she was doing well and by thirty she was rich. Her clients included pop stars, footballers, judges, members of parliament and even a bishop, and when her grandmother died she inherited most of her clients too.

It was therefore very inconvenient when she developed a bad case of Mediums' Block. Her mother couldn't work out why she'd got it. Nobody in their family had ever had it before. Was she sickening for something? The doctor said she was in perfect health. A broken heart? She'd never been in love. Was she missing Gran? Not really: they'd never been particularly close.

'Maybe she'd better consult a psychiatrist,' said Auntie Sue (who had several of them on her books).

'She's not going near one of those,' said Mo's mother heatedly. 'Bloody quacks the whole lot of them.'

'Then maybe she's just stressed. After all, the bereaved are a bit wearing if you get a lot of them at once. Look, why don't you go for reflexology? I've had this nice girl recommended. She specialises in occupational fatigue.'

'What's reflexology?' Mo wasn't up to date with complimentary therapies.

'Ooh it's lovely,' replied Auntie Sue. 'You just lie there on the bed and she twiddles your toes. You don't have to do exercises or anything, just smell the perfumes and let the music wash over you. It's ever so relaxing.

'But don't tell her what you do for a living,'

Auntie Sue continued. 'She might ask too many questions. Tell her you're a waitress and you're finding the customers a bit of a strain. It's the same thing really, they pay and you serve it up.'

'But doesn't she know you're a medium?'

'I've never met her; it was one of my clients who recommended her. She says she always gives her occupation as waitress when she doesn't want people to know what she does for a living.'

'Why on earth does she want to do that.'

'Because she's on the game, of course. All the girls in her house get stressed out; what with the things they're expected to do nowadays. Then they go for a spot of relaxation therapy and they're back on the job in no time.'

Mo made an appointment. She was looking forward to it; she couldn't wait to get something done about the problem that was threatening her livelihood.

She enjoyed the treatment. It was so relaxing lying peacefully on the bed having her feet gently massaged that she almost drifted off to sleep. Drowsily, she observed that the setting was not so very different from her own consulting room; subdued lighting, soft music and sweetly scented candles. Dimly, as in the distance, she heard her name being called.

'Yes?' she asked.

'Did you say something?' Said the therapist.

'I thought you called my name.'

'No, you must have been dozing a bit. People do. Just lie back and enjoy the treatment.'

Mo relaxed and shut her eyes. She heard her name called again, more strongly this time. She knew that voice, it was her grandmother! Her eyes flew open and she let out a startled yelp as she saw the old lady, as large as life peering over the therapist's shoulder.

'Sorry, did I hurt you?' The reflexologist looked contrite.

'No it's all right,' Mo replied, responding to a head-shake from her grandmother.

What on earth has that girl put in her burner, she thought, closing her eyes again. Mo didn't believe in spirits. It was all nonsense. She ought to know, she'd faked enough of them.

'Mo,' said the voice again. 'Lie still and listen. I don't want the therapist knowing I'm here; she'd only go asking questions. Just listen to what I tell you, because I won't tell you again.'

Mo glared at her grandmother through closed lids.

'And don't try arguing with me telepathically. I've got you where I want you for once; laid out all relaxed so you can hear me properly.'

'Nice and loose now,' said the therapist. 'Your feet are getting tense. Let them go, that's right.'

Mo relaxed obediently. She could still see her grandmother even though her eyes were closed.

Grandma looked cross. 'Mo, You've got to stop doing all that faking; it's not decent. You've got the power: it's time you got yourself an honest business. I didn't get to be top medium by making it all up, you know. Your mother's a fake and your Auntie Sue's a complete charlatan. Neither of them's got the talent; I'm ashamed of the pair of them, but you; you've inherited my gifts, so just you knuckle down and start learning to use them properly. You can get rid of that table knocker for a start. The spirits can't get a word in edgeways with all that noise going on.'

'And how am I supposed to do that?' Mo shot a thought towards her grandmother, though she still wasn't sure she believed in her.

'Relax and let your mind go blank of course, just like you're doing now. How do you think I got in here?'

Mo nodded speechlessly.

'Next time you do a séance, just breathe in and out deeply for a bit and let your thoughts drift off at random, and if any spirits want to come and comfort their loved ones you'll see them clearly enough. And that reminds me, the reflexologist's granddad wants to get in touch with you; here he is.'

Mo could see a shadowy form of an old man smiling at her over her Grandmother's shoulder. 'Tell my little girl not to worry about me, I'm very happy,' he said, then vanished.

'Don't you forget now,' said her grandmother, and vanished too.

The girl finished massaging Mo's feet. 'Do you feel better now?'

Mo nodded. And suddenly she realised that her Mediums' Block had gone. She was itching to get back to her parlour to try out her new found skills.

'Yes, I'm sure I can cope now. I've realised what I've been doing wrong, I've not been relaxing enough.'

'Oh good, but if you don't mind me saying so, I think you ought to pop along and see your doctor. You just might have something wrong in the Gynae. department; you let out quite a yell when I massaged the corresponding part of your foot. In your job you can't be too careful.'

'My job? However did you guess what I did?'

'Well it's not difficult is it. I get a lot of ladies telling me they're waitresses, but you can always tell a waitress; their feet get so sore and swollen'.

'Well seeing as you know, I might as well tell you that I've just seen your granddad.'

'What!'

'I've seen your granddad. He says you're not to worry about him, he's very happy.'

'You mean my granddad's been to see you?'

'Yes.'

'Why the dirty old man! Just wait till I tell my Gran what he's been up to.'

The therapist handed Mo her shoes abruptly, making her feel she was no longer welcome. It wasn't till she was almost half way home that she realised what the therapist must have thought she did for a living.

Then she remembered that people have two grandfathers!

The Paranoid Patient.

'Really Matron, Mr Enrico is getting more and more paranoid every day,' said Janet.

'What's he been saying this time?'

'Oh he's imagined seeing the window-cleaner again. He's sure the man's a secret agent come to "take him out" as he calls it.' Janet's soft brown eyes shone with exasperation. 'I know he can't help it but I wish he wouldn't go on and on. I've told him countless times that General Pinochet's regime has been out of power for years and in any case he's quite safe here in England.'

'Oh dear, I hope he hasn't upset the other residents again. Some of them are silly enough to believe him. I'll go and have a word with him myself.'

Matron bustled off to reassure the old man. This

would be the third time today she'd had to explain that The Pines didn't have strangers coming to clean the windows. Mark, their friendly handyman cleaned them all himself. I'll go and get him calmed down before his daughter gets here, she thought. I do hope he's not going to become confused again, he seemed so happy when he first came.

Mr Enrico's daughter was quite upset after she'd seen her father that afternoon, and called in at Matron's office to see if there was anything they could do to reassure the old man.

'I'm glad you came to see me,' said Matron, offering her tea. 'We've been rather concerned about your father. He's been worrying about an imaginary window-cleaner all this week. Have you any idea what's behind it?'

Mrs Brown shook her head. 'He'd always been quite sensible till about a month before we brought him here, even though he was so frail in other ways. Then one day the police rang me at work. One of the neighbours said that Father had come hammering on her door in his pyjamas, yelling that someone was after him, so she took him in and phoned the police. He said he'd gone for a lie down after lunch, then the window-cleaner had come up the ladder and was trying to get in to kill him. He got out of bed and ran out of the back door and along to my neighbour's house. The neighbour went round to investigate but by the time she got there the man with the ladder had gone.'

Matron nodded her head sympathetically. 'Do you think Mr Enrico imagined it?'

'I think he must have. The police checked all the window-cleaners in the district but none of them had been working in our street that day. Then they thought it might have been a burglar, but nobody reported anything missing. It seems as though Father just imagined the whole thing.'

'Could it have possibly had anything to do with your father's life in Chile? Was he in politics, or in some organisation that fell foul of the government?'

'No, I don't think so. We knew of course, that he didn't approve of the Pinochet regime; he often criticised it when he was safe in England with us. But he always said he'd kept out of politics. He didn't seem to have any difficulty in selling his business and transferring his money here, and they certainly didn't try to stop him leaving, so I don't suppose the regime had ever noticed him. He's never expressed any worries about Chile before and he's had no connection with the place for years.'

Mrs Brown finished her tea and continued. 'Then after the window-cleaner affair he became very disturbed. He wouldn't go out on his own. He'd go around testing all the doors and window locks even when we were at home with him and he positively shook with terror if he saw a stranger passing by. It was then that we decided we couldn't cope with him any more. For his own peace of mind we brought him here where there'd always be plenty of people around. We thought that would reassure him.'

'He seemed quite rational when he first arrived,' said Matron. 'We always thought him to be of above average intelligence. He could hold an interesting conversation and he used to help several of the ladies with their crossword puzzles. Then about a week ago he started to hide from strangers, and run up to the staff in terror, telling them that the window-cleaner was a secret agent out to kill him. But of course we don't have an outside window-cleaner, the handyman does them. The Doctor says Mr Enrico's got all the classical signs of Paranoia.'

Mrs Brown left, assured that the home would do all it could to keep her father happy, but worried about him nevertheless. He had fitted in very well when he first came to live with them, going out when it was fine, and staying indoors to enjoy a good read when the weather was bad. Then suddenly, he'd developed this quite unreasonable conviction that the secret police were after him.

Next time she visited, Mr Enrico's paranoia had worsened. He swore he'd seen the window-cleaner prowling around the grounds.

'Oh don't be silly Dad!' Mrs Brown was very embarrassed. 'You know you're safe here. There are people all around you. See, here's Janet come to bring the tea. She won't let anyone hurt you. And look, there's Mark mowing the lawn. I can't imagine anyone getting past Mark. He's very big and strong.'

Next morning, Mr Enrico felt unwell so Matron arranged for him to spend the day in bed. She'd got him nicely pacified by telling him that Mark was weeding the border just outside his window.

'Anyone trying to get up a ladder would have to go over Mark's head and I don't think he'd let anybody do that,' she said.

Matron put on her coat to go off duty and walked down the drive. Mark had moved over to the side border. She waved to him as she walked towards the gate.

Suddenly, out of the corner of her eye she noticed a ladder propped against the wall, reaching up to Mr Enrico's second-floor window and a man was climbing it!

She sprinted back to the house calling out to

Mark as she did so, then running indoors she hastily tried the lift, found it occupied and sped up the stairs two at a time. Janet coming down pulled back out of her way.

'Quick, come with me to Mr Enrico. There's something funny going on.'

They ran into the room just in time to see the figure silhouetted against the window point a gun at the old man on the bed, and fire.

Then there was a loud shout from outside. The figure at the window wavered, then disappeared. There was a thud, followed by another, and a loud scream.

Matron raced towards the bed. Mr Enrico lay there bleeding and groaning, and muttering to himself in some foreign language. She grasped a corner of the sheet and tried to stem the bleeding, though she knew it wasn't going to do any good.

'Call the ambulance!' She said. Janet ran off.

'I've called the ambulance and the police as well,' she said on her return.

'Then can you look outside and tell me what's happening down there.'

Janet opened the shattered window and leaned out. 'There's a man lying on the ground and Mark's got hold of him. I think the man's leg's broken; it seems to be lying at a funny angle. Oh, he's trying to fight Mark, even with that broken leg!'

Matron could hear sounds of a struggle from the garden, and a lot of cursing and yelling. Then she heard with relief, the howling of sirens and the clatter of apparatus being manoeuvred into the lift. She found her patient being taken from her as the paramedics tried unsuccessfully to save the old man. There was nothing more she could do here so she went to take charge of whatever was happening downstairs.

She found Mark in the entrance hall talking to a man in plain clothes who introduced himself as an Inspector from Special Branch. On the drive two uniformed policemen were dragging a man in overalls into a police car.

'I'm more sorry than I can say that you've had to put up with this incident,' said the inspector. 'Please reassure your old people that there will never be another incident like this again. But we're very very pleased that your handyman apprehended the gunman for us.'

'The man we've just arrested is a renegade Israeli secret agent. We know he's killed before but we couldn't pick him up because he hadn't committed a crime in this country. He's well known for tracking down ex-Nazi war criminals, so when we found out he was in the district we knew there had to be a war criminal at large, and naturally we wanted to get him too.'

'But he's killed Mr Enrico. He's not a Nazi, he's from Chile,' said Matron indignantly.

'He's not actually,' said Janet who had just come to join them. 'Mr Enrico's German. He was muttering all the time in German before he died, I know because I learnt German at school.'

'One of my residents a war criminal? I can't believe it.' Matron wrung her hands agitatedly. 'He seemed such a nice old man. The Israeli agent must have made a mistake.'

'I don't think he did, Matron. You see I could understand what Mr Enrico was saying. They were really horrible, the things he said.'

'What did he say?'

'He died cursing the Jewish people.'

Fairies at the Bottom of the Garden.

There are fairies at the bottom of our garden. I used to dance and sing with them when I was little and they taught me how to make daisy chains.

The houses in our lane have long gardens. At one time people grew their own vegetables and kept hens, but the town had grown outwards and swallowed up the village and the hens were long gone by the time my parents bought the property. Our garden was mostly laid to lawn and flower beds but there was a rough grassy plot at the bottom where we grew fruit trees. I used to go down the garden at dusk and wait beneath the old apple tree, then the fairies would come out from behind the blackcurrant bushes to sing and dance around me.

I never told anyone I played with the fairies. They were my own special secret and I knew I wouldn't be believed. I lost interest in them as my teens approached. I had far more exciting things to do. First it was ballet, then it was ponies and then of course, boys. Anyway, I never thought about them for years and I didn't even remember to go and say goodbye to them when I left home for college.

When I came home again that first summer I found my parents in a state of high anxiety and all the neighbours up in arms. The lane was under threat from property developers. Old Mrs Roseby had died and her nephew had sold her cottage to Ed Crotton, a nasty little speculative builder locally hated for the despoiling of Honeysuckle Corner.

Honeysuckle Corner had been a pretty little hamlet when I was small. My mother had had friends there and I'd loved visiting the picturesque old houses set higgledy-piggledy among the gardens. Then Ed Crotton bought a house. He'd told the seller it was for himself and his family to live in but as soon as the contract was signed, he'd sent in the demolition machines, knocked the house down and built four new houses on the site. The family next door found themselves looking into the back windows of some very ugly dwellings so naturally, they moved. Before they knew where they were the other residents of Honeysuckle Corner found themselves hemmed in, overshadowed and overwhelmed by the sort of house even a homeless family couldn't love. Everybody else sold out to the builder then, and now Honeysuckle Corner is a depressing little estate where people go when they can't afford anything else and they leave as soon as they can get a pay rise.

Now he was trying to do it again.

'Can't you get up a petition?' I said.

'We've tried,' said Dad. 'We got nowhere: the council wouldn't listen to us. Then we tried getting the local paper interested but they wouldn't even publish the letter.'

'They're all in it together,' said Mam. 'Builder, councillors, local rag, the lot. Ed Crotton's got relations on the council and shares in the local paper. There's nothing else we can do about it.'

Maybe *we* couldn't do anything about it but I knew who could. I waited for dark then went down the garden to talk to the fairies. I didn't know if they'd still want to talk to me now I'd grown up, and I wouldn't have blamed them if they didn't. After all, I hadn't bothered with them for years.

It was a still summer night. The moon lit a path for me and I could see the silhouette of the apple tree against the stars. I stood motionless, then began to sing one of the songs the fairies taught me. There was no echoing chorus from behind the blackcurrant bushes but I knew they were there.

'Listen,' I said. 'You probably won't want to talk to me now, but you must hear what I say or you won't have a garden to sing and dance in any more.'

There was no reply.

'Oh please listen. Ed Crotton's bought old Mrs Roseby's cottage and he's going to demolish it and build a lot more houses on the site. The people next door'll move and he'll do the same there and soon all the gardens will be built over and there won't be room for the fairies.

There was an angry rustle from the fruit bushes.

'Please help. We've done all we can but nobody will listen to us. There's only you can stop him now.'

There was no reply, but I knew that they'd heard me.

At seven o'clock the next morning a massive Hymac demolition vehicle rumbled up the lane and turned into old Mrs Roseby's gateway. Then it broke down. The workmen yelled and cursed but nothing they did could start it up again. Ed Crotton drove up and did a bit more yelling and cursing but even that didn't work, so he had to call out a mechanic from the hire company.

The man from the company came the next day but he couldn't find out what was wrong with the vehicle. He'd have to send to the manufacturers, he said. Unfortunately the manufacturers' head mechanic was away at a trade fair and wouldn't be back for three days; after which of course it would be the bank holiday.

Ed Crotton had a great deal to say over his mobile phone that day, and as it was hot weather and all the windows were open, the whole street enjoyed a good listen. Politely translated, his message was that he was paying £200 a day to hire the monster and he didn't think he was getting value for money.

The vehicle stayed there blocking the entrance for several days and Ed's costs must have been running into thousands. He tried to get it removed so that he could use a machine hired from another company, but the only man in the district with a vehicle big enough to tow away a Hymac was laid up indefinitely with a bad back.

My mother was batch baking for the freezer when we heard this latest piece of news.

'Can I have one of your cakes to give to some friends who're giving a party, Mam?' I asked.

'Surely. Would you like that one? It's the best,' she replied.

I took the best cake; a mighty affair layered with chocolate cream and with cherries on the top and put it on Mam's best china plate. I stole down the garden after dark and left the cake on the grass under the apple tree. There was a rustle from the bushes and I thought I heard a whispered 'yum-yum'.

'Thank you,' I said. 'I know you did something to the Hymac. Keep up the good work.'

The cake was gone the next morning, and someone had left a daisy chain on the plate.

The next night we had a very high wind and it blew down old Mrs Roseby's privy. It hadn't been used for years and had been boarded up and used to store garden tools. The kids next door climbed over the fence to go and look, even though they'd been they were told not to, and came screaming back home saying that there was a dead man down there. Their mother didn't believe them but she looked down the hole all the same, and saw a skull grinning up at her.

The police came and cordoned off the whole property, including the Hymac. Nobody else was allowed on the plot. Ed Crotton was furious. He'd found himself a mechanic by then.

'I'm paying two hundred pounds a day to hire that thing,' he yelled as he saw the tapes going up around his precious vehicle.

'This is a murder investigation Sir,' said the Inspector firmly. 'You'll just have to go and build something else till we're finished.'

I baked a batch of shortbread to give to the fairies and received another daisy chain in reply.

The police had no difficulty in identifying the victim; the local dentist recognised the skull as belonging to Larry Lamb. So did every other dentist in England. Larry had had some innovative work done to his jaw following a rugby accident and photographs of his teeth had made it into all the dental journals. The only problem was that Larry had last been heard of in Kathmandu.

Following a row with his girlfriend, Larry had packed his knapsack and gone off to Nepal some months ago. His parents hadn't really worried; he'd done it before and he'd always turned up safely. Now all they could tell the police was that they'd had a postcard from Kathmandu and heard nothing since.

The Nepalese authorities had no record of him and neither had the British consulate. Interpol became involved and the case dragged on for months.

Eventually, the police decided that there was no further evidence to be found in old Mrs Roseby's garden and took down the cordon. Unfortunately for Ed Crotton, one of the policemen was a keen amateur archaeologist, and had discovered many interesting artefacts when they were digging out the privy.

The site was much older than anyone had thought. In addition to the eighteenth century wine bottle, the Regency child's shoe buckle and the broken clay pipes in the privy itself, the constable had dug down far enough to find a couple of iron age artefacts in the stratum below. An expert was summoned, a site of special scientific interest declared and the area made off limits to everybody except the archaeology team.

Ed Crotton, who had finally managed to get his Hymac to start again, put the house back on the market and went off to build a supermarket in Saudi Arabia instead.

I made a pile of macaroons for the fairies this time. I didn't see them, but crunching noises accompanied me all the way back to the house and there was a massive daisy chain looped around the boughs of the apple tree next morning.

When the archaeologists had finally done with Mrs Roseby's garden, the agents sold the cottage to a nice young couple who fell in love with the roses round the door. They bought it well below its true value; skulls in the privy having a tendency to depress house prices. (The young couple didn't mind. They were both pathologists.)

That wasn't the end of the story though. The rest of Larry Lamb's body had never been found and the murder still hadn't been solved, when Larry's skull disappeared from the police laboratory. There were allegations of gross carelessness. A tough superintendent from another force came to investigate, and questions were asked in the House. Ed Crotton got his name in the papers too. He was caught drinking alcohol on a building site in Saudi Arabia and publicly flogged.

Then Larry Lamb turned up; not only alive and well but the acclaimed author of the latest best seller. He said he'd fallen unconscious in a village outside Kathmandu and some monks had taken him in and cared for him. He'd been ill for a long time and he'd had some weird hallucinatory experiences.

When he recovered he lodged with a farmer for a few months, doing a bit of work for his keep and writing an account of his strange adventures in his spare time. A friend in Kathmandu introduced him to a literary agent and Larry came back to England to collect a record advance from the publishers.

I saw him being interviewed on television.

'What were your out-body experiences like, Mr Lamb?'

'Oh strange; very strange. It seemed as though I was looking up at the universe through a round hole.'

'Looking *up*?' The interviewer's eyebrows moved upwards too. 'I would have thought that if you were floating on air you'd be looking down.'

Larry laughed. 'I wouldn't call it floating on air. It felt as though I was lying at the bottom of an old fashioned privy!'

Virus.

'The computer's not working Mr President.'

'Well get it working.'

'Even Professor Stanger can't get it working, Mr President.'

'Who?'

'He's the biggest expert on computers in the whole of the United States.'

'So get somebody else in then.'

'There isn't anybody else. We tried our own experts, then we tried the universities. Harvard and Yale both recommended Professor Stanger.'

'Have you tried the Pentagon?'

'Yes, Mr President. The defence experts couldn't get it working either.'

'So get some more computers. The Treasury can pay for them.'

'It's the Treasury computer that's down, Mr President. We can't pay anybody anything, not even our own salaries. The Government can't get at its own money. Somebody's planted a virus and until we get rid of it U.S. Treasury's kaput.'

'Goddam Ruskies!' yelled the president, banging on his desk. 'Send me General Hardanger. We'll blast 'em off the face of the Earth!'

President Samuel Starzenstruber had been elected on a patriotic ticket and couldn't get used to the Cold War being over. He'd be quite happy to despatch a few missiles to Moscow; particularly if it was done in time to get his salary back on line before pay-day.

Fortunately for the rest of the world, his Secretary of State didn't agree. Senator Roland Polanski had had a good relationship with the Russian Ambassador, even when the Cold War was still shivering.

Natasha Karsavina didn't want another cold war. She liked her comfortable embassy and nice friends among the international community. She liked the American way of life too; she could nip out for a burger, a bottle of Bourbon, or even a bar of soap at any hour of the day or night and go for an excellent cup of coffee afterwards.

So when Polanski telephoned and said could he

come and see her urgently, she flipped a few home-made cookies into the oven and got out the best china.

'Roly-Poly my dear,' she said, giving him an enthusiastic hug. 'How lovely to see you.'

'We've got to do something fast,' he said without preamble. 'The President wants to declare war.'

'He always does,' she said, refusing to be flustered. 'What is it this time?'

'The Treasury computer's down and he's blaming your government.'

'I thought computers were always going down.'

'This time it's not just down, it's totally non-functional. It's a virus and even Professor Stanger doesn't know what to do about it. The United States can't pay anybody for anything; we might as well be bankrupt.'

Natasha laughed delightedly – a rich deep grandmotherly laugh. 'The United States can't pay for anything? You mean that dollar imperialism is dead? You'll soon lose your standing in the free world if you cannot pay for it any more.'

'It's not funny Natasha. It means that nobody is going to get his salary this month. That's enough to set off a strike in government departments and the whole administration could collapse.'

'Maybe I could let you use our embassy

computer,' she said with a twinkle in her eye. 'Then we'd find out all your financial secrets. But seriously Roly, why don't you just persuade him to speak to Ivan on the hotline. I'm sure Ivan will convince the President it wasn't us.'

'We don't have the hotline anymore. The President had it disconnected as soon as he took office.'

Natasha raised her eyebrows. 'I wasn't told this. I had better speak to my government immediately.'

She left to speak to her government on the private line. She looked somewhat disconcerted when she returned.

'Ah, Roly-Poly my old friend, there is no need to declare war. Whoever has done this to you it is not Mother Russia. You see Roly – we had hoped not to have to tell anybody this – the Russian Treasury computer also is not working. There are those who blame your new President and others who think it must be one of our own rebelling provinces. We must convince our respective governments that we are both victims of the same enemy.'

Polanski chewed thoughtfully on his cookie. 'I'll have difficulty convincing the President. He thinks I'm a pacifist. I don't think he'll listen to me.'

'Then I shall talk to his wife. She asked me to attend one of her charity dinners recently and she'll think I'm returning the favour. But tell me, are any of your other computer programmes affected?'

'Fortunately, no.'

'Unfortunately, you mean,' she said grimly. 'If the defence computer's still working there'll be nothing to stop Sam Starzanstripes from setting off a few missiles.'

The Secretary of State paled beneath his tan. 'I'd better be getting back,' he said.

The United States and Russian presidents had hoped to keep their countries' problems secret as long as possible, and would probably have managed to do so at least until pay-day had not the Japanese announced their own computer failure. An international conference was called and all Washington hotels were put on alert for an influx of distinguished visitors. (Fortunately the travel industry's computers were unaffected.) For the first time in its history, every nation on earth, even the unofficial ones, sent a delegate. The fear of losing American aid is indeed a powerful motivator for international co-operation.

The first thing to emerge was that all the victims had found their computers disabled at the same time. The second was the discovery that nobody knew who was behind it. The third thing to emerge was that some countries were affected and not others. It was the immunity of some countries that provoked the most discussion, and a great many accusations.

The discovery that The United Kingdom had not been virused prompted an immediate accusation from President Starzenstruber. 'Them Limeys must'a done it to try and get their empire back,' he said.

It took a great deal of persuasion from the other delegates to stop him declaring war upon The Queen immediately.

All the African states were affected and accused the richer nations of racial discrimination. War nearly broke out in the Middle East when it turned out that every Arab state was affected but that Israel wasn't. Fortunately, Pakistan and Bangladesh were able to reveal that their undoubtedly Muslim nations were unaffected and that it therefore couldn't be a Zionist plot against Islam.

Who was behind it all remained a puzzle. There seemed to be no logic in the pattern of virus infestation. Neither geography, nor race, nor religion, nor any treaty or trade agreement could account for it. The whole of Africa was affected, whereas the Indian subcontinent was immune. In Europe, Germany and Italy were smitten, but

France was not. Australia had been targeted but New Zealand's treasury was still functioning. Size hadn't got anything to do with it either for both Iceland and Ireland were free of the nuisance.

The conference did the only thing it could; it set up a sub-committee. The sub-committee appointed a research team and Britain volunteered to host it at Cambridge in Professor Kelvin's faculty.

The United States sent Professor Stanger with the proviso that he wasn't to work with any Russians. Japan sent Mr Fujimoto, of Fujimoto Industries. Britain had originally intended to put Professor Kelvin in charge, but he said that as the matter was more about computer sabotage than computer programming they'd be better off with Dr Kenny.

Professor Stanger arrived early, just to make sure he was going to be the person in charge. Unfortunately for him Mr Fujimoto, who hadn't yet adjusted to the new time zone, was there even earlier. Dr Kenny, as befits an English academic, was ten minutes late.

'Damn Brits, can't even be here on time,' said Professor Stanger, venting his anger on the absent. He found someone else to vent it on a few minutes later when a young woman clad in jeans and tee shirt walked into the room carrying a file.

'I don't allow my secretaries to wear informal

clothing,' he said. 'Go home and put on some business clothes.'

The young lady's eyes flashed angrily. 'What you allow your secretaries is nothing to do with me. I am Dr Kenny from this faculty and I shall wear what I jolly well like.'

'Japanese women and children do not argue with men,' interjected Mr Fujimoto assuming that he was keeping the peace.

Dr Kenny controlled herself with an effort, and went towards her computer. 'I am authorised to get you anything you need for your researches, gentlemen,' she said. 'Have you any ideas about where you want to begin?'

They hadn't, but as she obviously had she sat down and began to search through some data immediately.

Professor Stanger got up and reached for the telephone, demanding to be connected to Professor Kelvin. 'Dammit, I'm not working with some *dame*,' he yelled. 'Send me some proper scientist immediately and stop fooling about with United States money or I'll see that we stop your foreign aid.'

'You forget yourself Professor,' Kelvin's voice boomed down the line. 'I'll excuse you this time as you've probably got jet lag, but I must remind you that it is *our* computer and *our* laboratory and we don't get American aid even when you *can* get at your own money.

'Besides, Isabel Kenny's the best hacker-cracker in Britain; probably in the whole world. She's been hacking into government computers since she was nine, and luckily for her, her parents found out and sent her to me for training. If anyone can discover who's behind it she can, so just you make sure you co-operate with her if you want to use my facilities.'

It didn't help that Mr Fujimoto laughed. Then he tried to exert his own authority by telling Dr Kenny to go and make the tea.

'The tea-boy will be around at ten thirty,' she said firmly. 'Now if you will both get on with your work I'll get on with mine.'

Three days later, none of the scientists had managed to get any further than the name of the virus, and that was only because the name kept flashing up on the screen.

'Virus Mariam, maybe it's a code name like Hurricane Hugo,' said Professor Stanger.

'It is probably a trade name in computer industry,' said Fujimoto.

Meanwhile, they worked. Isabel worked the hardest, but as she always left promptly at five, the men never suspected that she came back after dinner and worked till midnight, sometimes well beyond. She thought she might be able to sneak up on the hacker more easily without those two ham-fisted idiots alerting everybody to what they were trying to do.

She was fairly sure the hacker knew they were hunting him, for every now and then messages would flash momentarily onto the screen. They were always trivial and usually nonsensical, though occasionally she recognised a proverb or saying. A particular line from Shakespeare send Mr Fujimoto away to the library to hunt up the quotation, convinced that there must be a secret message hidden in it. A passage from the Declaration of Independence had similar effects on Professor Stanger. Isabel wasn't fooled; she just went on quietly tracking and tracking, until she was sure she had found the source of the messages she was getting.

'It's coming from somewhere in the Arabian Peninsula,' she said.

'I knew it was them damned Ay-rabs,' said Professor Stanger angrily.

'Then it must be terrorists. Japanese people do not treat with terrorists,' added Mr Fujimoto.

'Look, let's stop worrying about *why* they're

doing it and just track down *who* is doing it. I think I'm on to them. If we all share a round-the-clock watch I think we can pin them down, then maybe we can stop them.'

A few hours later, Isabel Kenny pushed back her chair and stretched. 'Gentlemen, I think we have them, but we mustn't let them know we know. We'll tell our respective governments, then I suggest we wait and see what else they do.'

They didn't have to wait for very long, for the very next day a message was received at the White House. A delegate would be coming to London (London England?) to discuss with the leaders of the G7 economies, the need to impose sanctions on countries that did not respect human rights. The messenger asked for a guarantee of immunity from arrest in return for an agreement to treat. It was given at once.

The Cambridge team pinpointed the source of the message as it was being sent. It came from one of the smaller Arab states.

'Possibly terrorists,' said the President's secretary.

'Well whoever they are, we know which plane they've booked their tickets on and as soon as they get there we'll arrest them.'

'I thought we gave them a guarantee of

immunity.'

'So we did. And if we break it, it'll learn them not to mess with Uncle Sam.'

The plans for arresting the hackers were put in place. The British government had been very co-operative. 'We don't negotiate with terrorists,' they said, as they sent the special branch to surround the airport. The Cambridge team continued to monitor the hackers. Easier now that they knew exactly where virus Mariam was coming from, the watchers could take it in turn to take a few hours off duty.

Isabel wandered idly through the city, blinking in the unaccustomed sunlight. She didn't feel like eating and she was too keyed up to go home and snatch a few hours sleep. She wandered into the library and began to browse. She lifted up a book from the in-shelf and flicked idly through it. It was a silly romance, so she put it down and took up another.

She found she was holding in her hand a copy of the Koran. She'd never read it before. Maybe she should read through it – it might give her some insight into Middle Eastern attitudes. She flicked through the pages, not finding it easy to understand. Then she paused, for one of the chapters was headed "The Book of Mariam".

She sat down to read it. It didn't take long, for it

covered only a couple of pages. But it was the story of Mariam herself that surprised her, for it was essentially the story of the Annunciation as told in the Gospel of St Luke.

Mariam, The Blessed Virgin Mary, the only woman to have conceived without the aid of man. Could the virus have been devised by some sort of feminist group? Things started to click into place. Why had Britain been immune and America not? Why France but not Germany, New Zealand but not Australia? Why Iceland, Ireland, Sri Lanka, Israel?

Because each of those countries had had a woman head of state, of course!

Things were becoming clearer now. Could Mariam be the code name for a group of Arab women campaigning for women's rights? And did they really think they could blackmail the rest of the world into imposing sanctions on nations who didn't believe in them? Surely not; the Arab states were awash with oil and could hold the rest of the world to ransom any time they liked.

Or could they?

She ran to the reference section. "The Arabian Peninsula is lacking in practically every natural resource except oil. The Arab states have to import 90% of their food and raw materials."

'Oh yes, we could boycott them all right if the

will were there,' she thought. 'They'd starve sooner than we ran out of oil. But is the will there?'

Probably not, she thought to herself ruefully. She just couldn't imagine the British government, let alone America, Russia and Japan imposing sanctions on countries it wanted to trade with just because they wouldn't give their women the vote. Mariam's delegates would be arrested at London airport and the Emirate and its disgraceful associates would get away scot-free as usual. She shuddered to think what might happen to the women who had planted the virus if they were handed back to their own country. Flogging? Mutilation? Beheading even? She couldn't let it happen. She wasn't going to let it happen. She'd be in time to stop them; she *must* be in time to stop them!

The laboratory was empty. Professor Stanger and Mr Fujimoto had gone for a sleep. Hastily she turned on her computer. They wouldn't have left for the airport yet. Warn them; warn them first, she thought as she tapped out a message. Then she dialled up alternative flights. She'd arrange for them to enter the country some other way and she'd meet them and take the message for them to the rendezvous.

The Reception committee at Gatwick airport

intercepted every passenger from the flight that arrived at eleven o'clock that evening, and caused a great many diplomatic incidents in the process. Arab princes do not like being asked their business when they arrive anonymously in London at night. Neither do businessmen who come to do deals that the Government hopes to keep from the press. Threats of another oil crisis vied with promises to renege on arms deals in embassies and police stations throughout London that night. Nobody who could have been from the Mariam group was apprehended.

Meanwhile, the computers of all affected countries bore the message "Mariam Rules OK" superimposed across a picture of the Annunciation.

Isabel went to Stanstead airport in the small hours, waiting for the plane from Paris. It was late, and she nearly missed the three black-robed and veiled ladies who emerged just as she was nodding off. She jumped to her feet just in time to greet them.

'Good evening Mariam,' she said.

'Good evening Sister,' said three ladies in unison.

She hastily escorted them to her car. They exclaimed in surprise at its smallness. They exclaimed in surprise again when they saw the small motel room she had booked for them. 'We usually stay at the Ritz,' said one who seemed to be the leader. 'Why can't we go to the Ritz?'

'Wouldn't you be recognised?' said Isabel.

'In this outfit?' There was a gale of laughter from the other two.

'I shall book in as Mrs Ahmed.'

'We shall all book in as Mrs Ahmed.' Another gale of laughter.

The eldest lady picked up the phone and booked four rooms at the Ritz. 'I want rooms with a computer and Internet access,' she said firmly, as the other two stripped off their black outfits and dressed themselves in designer jeans and glamorous tops. 'We shop by Internet,' explained the lady who looked about fifteen. The eldest lady finished her phone call and pulled on a couturier day dress. 'Now can we take a taxi?'

'I don't have enough money for a taxi to London,' said Isabel, who was feeling a little overwhelmed by this show of wealth.

They thought this hilarious. Arab ladies take taxis everywhere, it seemed.   Isabel got to know the three women very well on the journey to London. Ayesha was the eldest, she said. She'd asked her husband for computing lessons as a wedding gift and he'd sent to America for a woman teacher for her. Then she'd taught Fatima and Zuleika when

116

they joined the household.

'Are you all married to the same man?' Isabel thought she'd better get that clear.

Another ripple of laughter. 'English women do not think about husbands the way we do.'

'How will your husband feel about you leaving home?' Isabel asked.

'He won't care; he's just taken another wife.' Another ripple of laughter. 'But I told him we would all like to go to Amman to see my sister's new baby. In Jordan women may go about freely, so when we had seen the baby we took a flight to Paris and came on here.'

Ayesha had booked another room for Isabel. She insisted on paying for it. 'We know what salary you get; it is not enough for the Ritz.'

Isabel raised her eyebrows.

'We know what salary everybody gets. Did you know that Professor Stanger and Mr Fujimoto have been promised a bonus of a million dollars by the American government for tracking down the virus but that you are only getting five thousand?'

She didn't know.

Ayesha, safe in her anonymity at the Ritz sent a stern e-mail to President Starzanstruber, instructing him to declare sanctions against all countries that did not give full civil rights to women. Naturally he refused, so Mariam knocked out the Pentagon, The Oval Office, a rather shady company the President had interests in and Disneyland too, just for good measure. The rest of the G7 economies suffered similar fates, even those previously unaffected. By the end of the morning, parliaments, senates, despots, dictators and religious fanatics had all capitulated.

Women had the vote, the right to own property, the right to consent to marry and the right to drive a car, all over the world. Mariam made sure everyone knew that if any nation tried to backtrack on its women's rights, or if Mariam's delegates were not alive and free to override it at frequent intervals, another and far worse virus would cripple the world's treasuries. As an added incentive, Mariam published a few scandals involving world leaders on the Internet just as a warning of what she could do. Some governments fell.

The Cambridge team was invited to Washington for a final conference. Isabel's new friends interrupted their buying spree just long enough to say goodbye and present her with a Cartier watch. When she went to the bank for some spending money she was surprised to find her account had been credited with two million and five thousand dollars from the United States Treasury.

She was ignored throughout the conference. Stanger and Fujimoto spent the time alternately vying with each other for the credit in tracking down the Mariam virus and accusing the U.S. Government of not paying them the promised bonuses. The U.S. Treasury for its part wasted a lot of time insisting that the bonuses had been paid. Mariam's escape from capture was not referred to as it would have meant admitting that the world's heads of state had gone back on their word.

Isabel was therefore surprised to receive an invitation to tea and cookies at the Russian embassy.

'My dear Dr Kenny, I am so pleased to be able to speak freely to you at last.' Natasha Karsavina favoured her with a warm maternal smile. 'And I have a small present for you. It is only a copy but it is a good one.' She handed her a small silver-framed icon of the Annunciation.

'I know it was you who found out where the virus was coming from. I too know a little about computers – enough to know that those others got to where they are by plagiarism of other people's work. And I know too that it was you who stopped them from taking Mariam a prisoner. It was an Arab woman wasn't it?'

Isabel said nothing. She hadn't told anyone she'd

met the three women hackers.

'Oh I do not blame you my dear, for I know they intended to seize them and imprison them, maybe even hand them back to their own countrymen to terrible punishments. If I had known what you knew I would have done the same.

'And you should not wear that Cartier watch so openly. I cannot be the only person in Washington who knows what they cost.'

'How did you know it was I who warned them, Madame Karsavina?'

The Russian chuckled. 'We had several Islamic states in the Soviet Union. Islam does not like pictures and statues of prophets and saints. A Muslim woman would not have thought to put an icon of The Holy Virgin on the computer screen. That message could only have come from you'

Haunting the Aisles.

The trouble with being a ghost in a National Trust property is that you can only frighten people in the summer months because all the stately homes are closed for winter. This didn't please the spectres of Sputtering Hall.

'I'm bored,' said Lord Charles, the laughing cavalier who loved frightening the ladies.

'And I'm tired of playing the spinet to an empty room.' Lady Clorinda didn't like being alone; it made her feel unwanted.

'I'd just go to bed till springtime,' interjected Cousin Jamie in a world-weary voice. 'Only unhallowed ground is so cold and damp and full of creepy crawlies.'

The trio hung about the house disconsolately.

'It's not fair,' said Lady Clorinda. 'If we'd all had the Christian burials we were entitled to we wouldn't have had to haunt this horrible hall till doomsday.'

The others nodded sympathetically. The two men had had their bit of fun before being consigned to their unhallowed graves, but poor Clorinda, prevented from marrying her handsome gardener, had pined away in despair and been hastily interred in an unconsecrated bit of the family churchyard. She spent the next two centuries haunting the withdrawing room, endlessly playing the spinet – which was very clever of her as the Curator kept it locked.

Lord Charles, as befits a man named after the Merry Monarch, had always believed in enjoying himself. His revels came to an end when the miller caught him with his daughter and attacked him with the grain shovel. Seeking escape by diving into the millpond, he hit his head on the bottom and drowned. The Vicar, who assumed he'd killed himself in an attack of remorse, refused him a Christian burial and his father had to bribe the under-gardener to bury him in the orchard. A pale shadow of his former self, he still felt attracted to the ladies and made a point of lurking in places he was fairly certain he could catch them alone.

There was some mystery about the death of Cousin Jamie. A new bride coming to Sputtering

Hall insisted upon bringing her orphaned cousin with her. Tongues wagged, and when a few days later his body was found hanging from a beam in the bathroom, he was assumed to have killed himself out of unrequited love. His coffin was buried at the cross-roads but his spirit returned to the Hall, where visitors frequently bumped into him hanging about in dark corners.

One miserable autumn day when the ghostly trio would have died of boredom had that still been possible, Lady Clorinda faced the two men and said, 'I've got to get out of here.'

'Can we?' said Lord Charles.

'I don't know see why not. Cousin Jamie comes up here every day from the cross-roads.'

'Well there's nothing else to do down there any more,' said Jamie petulantly. 'Nobody goes past since they diverted the road to build a supermarket.'

It took a while to explain to the other two what a supermarket was.

'Have you ever been inside it?' Lady Clorinda wanted to know.

Jamie shook his head. 'I don't like newfangled things much.'

'Well let's go and take a look at it. I haven't been in a shop for ages.' Lady Clorinda brightened up for the first time since she'd scared a schoolgirl silly in

September.

The men nodded in agreement (although Cousin Jamie couldn't do it without wobbling) then they all trooped down the road to the supermarket, frightening a few motorists into the ditch on the way. They slipped invisibly through the door.

'Gosh,' said Lady Clorinda. 'Isn't it light in here. Where is it all coming from? I can't see any candles.'

'Magic!' exclaimed Cousin Jamie, who was a little superstitious. 'I don't want to stay. Let's get out of here.'

'Don't be silly,' said Lord Charles crossly. 'Nothing can hurt you; you're dead.' He'd just seen a gaggle of schoolgirls coming in for cigarettes and couldn't wait to start putting on a performance.

'I like it,' said Lady Clorinda suddenly. 'Let's spend the winter here. It's lovely and warm; there's lots going on and plenty of people to terrify. We never get as many visitors as this at Sputtering Hall.'

The others agreed and began haunting immediately. Lady Clorinda clung around the chiller cabinet putting people off the cream cakes. Sales fell dramatically but the manager couldn't understand why. The Sputtering spectres had long since learnt to get around without being spotted by people in authority.

Lord Charles had a marvellous time haunting the ladies' cloakroom. The loos, fully automated and disability friendly, did everything for the customer from opening the door when she went in to washing her hands afterwards. The appearance of a ghostly cavalier among the automatic flushes and invisible blasts of hot air had a deleterious effect on customer morale, and the shoppers very quickly took their custom elsewhere.

Cousin Jamie, who found the bright lights and crowds too much for his sensitive nature, haunted the waste paper skip in the car park. Environmentally conscious citizens depositing yesterday's news reacted delightfully to the sight of his strangulated features and dropped the lid with a most satisfying clang. He hadn't enjoyed himself so much in years, and as the skip was right on top of his grave, he could nip home quickly when anything upset him.

The customers deserted in droves, though they didn't say why. Though one may safely admit to having seen a ghost in a stately home without losing credibility, nobody's going to risk ridicule for spotting a spectre in a supermarket. Profits fell and the manager was threatened with the sack.

It was the Vicar who saved his bacon. She'd just

arrived in the parish; and after serving as chaplain to a psychiatric prison, was totally unshockable.

She was surprised to see Cousin Jamie when she deposited her old newspapers in the skip, but not too alarmed. She was used to coming across suicides in unlikely places.

'How odd, I must be imagining things,' she said to herself. 'The doctor did warn me I might get repercussions. Oh well, better forget it and carry on with the shopping.'

She went inside and began to fill her trolley. But when she caught sight of Lady Clorinda pottering around the patisserie she knew she couldn't be hallucinating.

'Ghosts!' she exclaimed. 'I can't be having two repercussions in one supermarket. I'll inform the Manager then go and telephone the Diocesan Exorcist.'

She knew the Exorcist well; he'd often called at the prison.

'Better pop in here first though, these things can go on a long time,' she said as she went into the ladies' room.

She wasn't at all pleased to find Lord Charles attempting to share it with her.

'Out!' She snapped in the tone of voice she'd always used with intrusive inmates.

He fled.

The Diocesan Exorcist was delighted to hear from the Vicar; he'd been looking for an excuse to see her again. He arranged to meet her at the supermarket at closing time and hoped she'd to go out to dinner with him afterwards.

The Manager agreed to the ceremony and though he said he didn't believe in ghosts, he slipped a few garlic bulbs into his pocket when he thought nobody was looking.

The Exorcist arrived in full clerical paraphernalia and took bell, book and several official looking candles out of his briefcase.

'Now come out, all of you,' he said to the empty aisles.

The three spectres materialised.

'What do you think you're doing, haunting this supermarket?'

They all began talking at once.

'One at a time please. Let the cavalier go first; he seems to be the oldest. You can't have died here: where do you really come from?'

'Sputtering Hall,' Lord Charles replied.

'And why didn't you stay there?'

'Because there's nobody to frighten in winter.'

'Then why don't you go back to your graves till summer comes?'

'Because we're buried in unconsecrated ground and there's nothing to do down there.'

'And I get so cold and lonely.' Lady Clorinda began to sniffle.

'I can't stand the creepy-crawlies,' Cousin Jamie added lugubriously.

'Why aren't you buried in consecrated ground? One at a time now; ladies first.'

'They said I'd deliberately starved myself to death because my father wouldn't let me marry the gardener. But I didn't; I just couldn't eat because I felt so miserable.' Lady Clorinda began to cry in real earnest.

'Anorexia Nervosa,' said the Vicar authoritatively. 'I saw a lot of it on the Neurosis Wing.'

The Exorcist nodded.

'Now you Sir,' he pointed to Lord Charles.

'I drowned escaping from an angry father. They said I'd committed suicide in a fit of remorse, silly devils. What on earth would I want to do that for?'

'And what about the young man with the hangdog expression?'

Cousin Jamie looked mutinous. He might have been hanged, but he objected to having his expression likened to that of a dog.

'My cousin's husband murdered me,' he said

128

sulkily. 'Then he told the magistrate I'd hanged myself out of unrequited love for his wife.'

The Exorcist was dying to know if he'd ever requited it but didn't like to say so in front of the Vicar. He whispered a while with his colleague, then turned to the three ghosts again.

'You're to quit this supermarket forthwith. I'm about to exorcise you, then you'll go to Eternal Rest.' He handed the Manager a candle and took a small spray bottle out of his briefcase.

'Can't we just go back to Sputtering Hall?' Lord Charles didn't care for the thought of having holy water squirted all over him.

'No you can't. You're a trio of thoroughly irresponsible ghosts, ruining this poor man's business with your silly antics.'

They hung their heads in shame.

'Oh I did so want to rest in consecrated earth,' gulped Lady Clorinda between sobs.

'Show me where your grave is and I'll come along and bless it.' The Vicar felt quite sorry for the girl. 'Just let me go and get my things.'

'And I'll come and help you.' The Exorcist wasn't going to let the Vicar out of his sight now that he'd found her again.

The ghosts led the way and the clergy prayed them into their graves – though the Manager had to help them shift the skip off Cousin Jamie's first

After that, the Sputtering Spectres rested in peace; or of they didn't nobody ever found out, for they were never seen again.

Visitors to Sputtering Hall were cross when they didn't see any ghosts that summer. People may not like being frightened, but they have a wonderful time telling everybody about it afterwards.

But the Hall wasn't left unhaunted for long. A visiting American, appalled at British eating habits, had thrown a fit of apoplexy and died. Now he haunts the cafeteria extracting the kidney from the steak and kidney pies, slurping ketchup onto the Yorkshire puddings and worst of all, chilling the beer so cold that English people's insides curl up with the shock of it. Fortunately, The Hall doesn't open in winter: chilled beer in December would have killed the locals stone dead.

Postman's Knock.

Mike slammed the door behind him and rushed off into the rain. The post was late, but he'd waited, hovering anxiously beside the door even though he must have known it would make him late for work. Sarah had never known Mike be late for work before. There could only be one explanation; her husband was seeing another woman.

He'd been acting oddly lately, hanging around for the post every day, scanning each envelope briefly but often not bothering to read his mail until he came home. Sarah and Mike had always shared everything; money, responsibilities, joint bank account, and they'd always left sorting the post to whoever got there first. Now Mike seemed reluctant to let her see the mail till he'd checked it over. Clearly he was hiding something and she could only think that he must have been getting love letters. There was no other explanation.

He'd been saving his money too, so he must be spending it on the other woman. They'd always been open with each other about money before. They both had their own allowances in addition to the housekeeping and Mike's expenses, then they'd laugh and lend each other a pound or two if the other ran out of money before pay-day.

They'd had to budget carefully since Mike had lost his job and had to take lower paid work, but with a bit of planning and common sense they didn't go short of the essentials. They'd skipped the holiday this year and made do with days out instead and Sarah hadn't bought any new clothes, but then she hadn't really needed any. The biggest economy had been the car. Mike had always used it to get to work. Now he walked, and except when he had to drive to head office in Newcastle, only took the car when it was raining. Well today was raining fit to drown a whole pondful of ducks, yet Mike had simply donned his mac and gone off on foot.

He'd been economising on lunches too. He'd always said that one of the good points about his new job was the canteen, but now he'd suddenly started taking sandwiches. Sarah had come down one morning and been surprised to find him buttering bread and slicing cheese.

'What on earth are you doing?' she'd said.

'I'm making sandwiches. I'm getting a bit sick of the canteen; you can tell what day of the week it is by the menu.'

Sarah sympathised. It must be just like school dinners, she thought, being expected to eat the same dish the same day of the week year after year. She'd offered to get up earlier and make them for him but he'd refused.

'You've enough to do with the baby,' he'd said.

So she'd let it go at that.

There'd been other little economies too. No pay-day tube of Smarties for little Jo and he hadn't brought home the magazine he particularly liked, or his favourite bottle of real ale recently. She kicked herself when she remembered that she'd thought he must be saving up to give her a nice surprise for her birthday – a food processor perhaps – but her birthday had been and gone with nothing more than the usual bottle of perfume. That really proved he was saving his money to spend on somebody else.

Sarah strapped the baby into the buggy and set off for the playgroup. She'd have liked to confide in somebody, but who? Though she got on well with the other mums, she didn't have a close friend among them. Normally she'd have rung her mother who was marvellous at putting things into perspective, but Mam was very preoccupied just now. Gran had broken her hip and needed regular visiting to cheer her up, and someone had to keep an eye on the house and water the plants while she was in hospital. Gran's plants were her pride and joy; she won prizes with them.

'You're my pride and joy', Sarah said to the children as she wheeled them the short distance through the rain, for it wasn't worth getting the car out to go a couple of blocks.

'What's pride and joy, Mam?' said Jo.

'It means you're very special,' she replied, then with a sudden shiver she realised she wasn't special to Mike any more.

She couldn't keep her mind on the playgroup today; it kept wandering off wondering how she'd cope. Should she confront him? She didn't know how. How do you say; 'Are you having an affair?' to someone you've always loved and trusted? What would she do if he said yes, divorce him? Should she make a scene or bear it nobly and impress everybody with her fortitude? She didn't think she could muster up very much fortitude at the moment while her whole life was being pulled out from under her.

She could of course go and find the other woman

and have it out with her, but what would she say? 'I gather you're having an affair with my husband and will you please just stop it.' Somehow she didn't think that would work either.

'Sarah, what are you doing? Jo's nearly fallen off the climbing frame!' The playgroup leader's voice cut into her thoughts and brought Sarah back to reality with a jolt.

She thought about divorce again when she'd taken the children home and tucked them up for their nap. She didn't want a divorce. The lady over the road had had a divorce and they'd had to sell the house and share out the possessions. They'd had to share the children too and Sarah knew she couldn't bear that. Surely the court wouldn't take her children away from her? No of course they wouldn't. Jo and the baby were much younger than the children in the other family, but maybe she'd have to let them go to their Daddy at weekends. No, she could never let that happen to her.

Perhaps she'd better go and see a matrimonial counsellor instead and find out what to do to save her marriage. Sarah cried a little then. The thought of having to tell someone that Mike had been unfaithful was too much to bear. She imagined the counsellor looking coldly at her and blaming her for her husband's infidelity.

Tears rolled down her cheeks and it wasn't until she heard the key turning in the door that she realised she'd wasted the whole afternoon thinking miserable thoughts. Hastily she ran to the sink and pretended to be washing out the feeding cup, though of course she'd done it as soon as she'd fed the baby. Mike came in and kissed the top of her head, then ran upstairs to change, and by the time he'd come down she'd managed to get her face in order again.

She prepared a meal of egg and chips for she'd forgotten to shop for the evening meal. Mike didn't seem to notice anything amiss and just sat watching the television till bed time. Sarah couldn't sleep, tossing and turning as she racked her brains trying to think of some way out of the situation.

The sky was starting to lighten when the idea came to her. She'd get the evidence, then decide what to do; she was going to make sure that she read the mail first that morning. She rose quietly and felt beside the bed for Mike's shoes then crept downstairs with them and hid them behind the washing machine in the utility room. She took the spare pair from the hall cupboard and hid them too, then slipped back into bed without waking Mike.

Next morning her husband called out as she cooked the breakfast, 'I can't find my shoes, have you seen them?'

'No, not recently. Come and have your breakfast, you can look for them afterwards.'

Then when Mike was searching the bedroom again, it was simplicity itself to nip outside with a cloth and pretend to be wiping something off the window while she waited for the postman to arrive. As soon as he came she took the letters and hid them under her apron, then ran indoors again and retrieved Mike's shoes from where she'd hidden them.

'I've found your shoes in the utility room,' she called. 'Hurry, or you'll be late.'

'There's no post for us today,' she added as her husband bent down to tie the laces. 'I just saw the postman go past.' She felt guilty about the lie.

Mike gave her a quick kiss and departed for work, and as soon as he'd gone, she locked herself in the bathroom to read the mail. Throwing aside the special offers and charity appeals, she ripped open the big white envelope addressed in a feminine hand.

"You have been specially chosen to receive our latest offer," it said. She flung it from her in disgust. It was nothing more than an advertisement for double glazing made up to look like a personal letter.

She left the manila envelope till last. It would be a bill and she'd deal with it later. Funny though, there weren't any bills due this month. What on earth could it be? Unless of course Mike's other woman worked in an office and used the office stationery for her love letters!

Suddenly, she couldn't bear to look. Jo was calling her and the baby was crying. She thrust the envelope down behind the cistern and went to her children.

It was not till after lunch that Sarah could steel herself to look at the letter. Should she steam it open so Mike wouldn't know that she'd seen it? But no, she'd never steamed a letter open in her life. She'd open it properly then admit to what she had done.

She took a knife and slit the envelope neatly along the top seam. It contained a single page of official looking writing.

"Northumbria Police Authority" it announced in its sinister black print. "We have photographic evidence that you were the driver of a vehicle exceeding the 30 mile speed limit on 27th February at 15.45 p.m."

Sarah laughed aloud in relief. There hadn't been another woman after all! Mike didn't want her to see the mail because he'd just been fined for speeding. He must have been caught by a speed camera last time he went to Newcastle, and been saving like mad ever since to pay the fine without having to take the money out of the joint account, where she'd have been sure to notice.

'That'll learn him!' she said loudly to the tiles and cistern, with a flash of resentment against all the misery that his secrecy had put her through. He'd have to be less supercilious about her driving too now, she thought. He'd taught her to drive and never quite lost his superior attitude. 'Typical man,' her Mam had said. 'If we won the Grand Prix at Monte Carlo every year they'd still think they were better drivers than us.'

But why did he keep it a secret? Surely he knew she wouldn't crow. Well maybe she would crow – just a bit – and serve him right for not telling her. She chuckled a little at the thought of his face when she confronted him with the letter.

Sarah showered and put on her best dress to welcome her husband home that evening. She'd bought him a bottle of real ale from the off-licence and served it with his favourite steak and kidney pie. Then when she'd got him nicely settled into the living room with his cup of coffee, she pounced.

'This came for you this morning from the Northumbria Police Authority,' she said.

Mike gave a squawk of embarrassment and snatched it from her.

She grinned.

'Naughty boy,' she said.

'I was only doing forty-two,' he said defensively. 'It was on that bit outside Newcastle where you don't realise it's a thirty-mile limit. Lots of people get caught there.'

'Can we afford the sixty pounds?' Sarah couldn't resist turning the knife a little.

'It won't come out of the account, I've been saving up out of my own money.'

'Have you got some little crosses on your driving licence too?' said Sarah sweetly.

Mike nodded miserably.

Then Sarah reached behind her to bring something out from behind the sofa cushion.

'Me too,' she said, producing another letter headed "Northumbria Police Authority". 'I got this last month when I drove up to see Gran in Sunderland.'

There'll Always be an Arthur

Mum put the phone down and smiled. 'We've an American coming to stay tomorrow. He wants to stay the week – says he's doing some research on King Arthur.'

'I'm surprised there's any left to do,' said Dad. 'I thought that particular seam had been worked out years ago.'

'Don't knock it,' Mum said. 'We don't often get them for the whole week.'

This was true. When you're mainly a farm and the guesthouse comes second you mostly get passing trade; a night or two at a time before they go on to the next attraction.

'What's his name?'

'I didn't catch it. Something P. Something; very American. I hope he gets on all right with Arthur.'

'Why shouldn't he get on all right with Arthur? Arthur likes people, especially if they make a fuss of him.'

'He doesn't like foreigners.'

'Arthur doesn't like foreign cats.'

This also was true. Arthur was the sort of cat who didn't care much for having other cats on his territory at the best of times, but the sight of a slinking Siamese or a waddling rug of a Persian would send him into paroxysms of rage. We needed Arthur. He was the best ratter in the district and we couldn't afford to offend him.

Arthur, though undoubtedly healthy, was frankly, ugly. Big and square, he had a pugnacious nose and frayed ears. Furthermore, as though being white with Dalmatian spots wasn't enough, he had a crooked smudge on his nose that made him look as though he was permanently scowling.

Arthur's feelings apart, Mum was quite excited at the thought of having an American visitor. She'd always wanted to visit the United States but the farm just wasn't making the sort of money to allow for long trips. A week in Cornwall was about all we could ever afford and she had to console herself with reading all about the USA instead.

'He's hired a car,' she said. 'I do hope he'll be all right on these country lanes. They have very good roads in America.'

'Did you warn him not to arrive around four? We don't want him to be stuck in the cow-jam.'

We have famous cow-jams in Glastonbury and Dad was always a bit dismissive of visitors' ability to negotiate our twisty Somerset roads.

He needn't have worried. The visitor arrived just in time for tea and introduced himself as Felix P. Litterschratter.

Mr Litterschratter looked just like an American should. He was tall and tanned, with a squarish face and close-cropped fair hair. He wore a very nice pair of khaki trousers and a quiet shirt; just like the visiting preachers who sometimes came to the chapel.

He addressed Dad as Sir and Mum as Ma'am and soon made a good impression. He liked English tea, he said, and complimented Mum on her flans and malt loaf, saying it was a long time since he'd enjoyed such good home cooking.

We needn't have worried about him finding any Arthurian relics to research. His ideas of that period of history were pure Hollywood. Dad gaped open-mouthed as our guest rattled on about Sir Lancelot and Queen Guinevere; and did we really think that the Lady of the Lake had lived around here? Mum gave Dad a warning look. She didn't want him arguing and spoiling what promised to be a very easy week's money. Felix P. had already shown a willingness to do practically everything for himself and he'd offered Mum another five pounds a day if he could have dinner with us. He was tired of restaurants, he said.

Arthur took to him at once, running up to mew a greeting as soon as he arrived, then sitting quietly at his feet while he had his tea. Mr Litterschratter seemed a little puzzled at our choice of name.

'Surely you don't call your cat after one of your heroes?' He said.

It took Dad a while to find a reply to that. We take King Arthur pretty much for granted round here; it's only the tourists and weirdoes who make a big thing about him. After all, he may not even have existed.

'There's always been an Arthur on the farm,' Dad said. 'My father had one and his father before him, and it's always been a white cat with black spots and a smudge on his nose. Whenever one cat dies somebody always seems to have another spotted kitten to give away so's we can always replace him.'

The reigning Arthur jumped up on Mr Litterschratter's knee at this point and our guest was very flattered. We hadn't the heart to tell him that

Arthur just likes sitting on knees and any old pair will do.

Felix P. went off for a walk along the lane after tea. He'd been very disappointed to be told that the lake the lady had lived in was no more.

'How come the authorities let anyone destroy such a valuable piece of history?'

'For the same reason that Americans destroyed so much of their own environment, Money,' said Dad tartly.

Then he relented (having been given a dirty look by Mum) and told him how the marshes had been drained centuries ago but that in heavy rain, the lake would come back for a few days till it drained away again. Dad got out the map and showed him where the mere had been, then sent him off happily to go and search for it.

Our guest came home looking pleased with himself and said he'd found traces of a ruined building that he'd photographed. We didn't tell him it was just the remains of an old barn; though I suppose it could have been Tudor or even Mediæval as far as we knew.

He went on at length about the lady of the lake then screwed up his face and asked, 'But what is that building on the other side of the lane about a quarter mile away? It smells terrible.'

'The one that looks like a farm; red brick with tiled roofs and a long low barn?'

'Yeah, that's the one. It smells like they got a few skunks holed up in there.'

Mum laughed. 'Not skunks, just a few tomcats. It's a stud farm for pedigree Cornish Rex; dreadful looking things always getting out and yowling all over the neighbourhood. We don't like them because they crossbreed with our decent ratters then we get all sorts of odd-looking kittens in the litters. You can always tell when one of those things has been around.'

'And Arthur always sends them packing!' chipped in Dad laughing.

Arthur, hearing his name mentioned, stood up and purred right in Mr Litterschratter's face and rubbed against his cheek. Felix P. was hooked.

The next day, Dad sent our guest off to Glastonbury sure that he'd find plenty of ammunition for a good wallow around in myth and legend, and with the name of a good pub for lunch. He arrived home just in time for dinner, looking as though he'd thoroughly enjoyed himself.

'How did you like Glastonbury?' Mum asked as soon as she'd served him.

'Great, Great! It's kinda strange though. There sure are some funny people about.'

Mum laughed. 'It certainly does attract some oddly dressed tourists in the summer. But surely you enjoyed the Abbey and the old churches? And there's lots of interesting things to do and see around the town.'

'But gee, you even have a Goddess Temple. I'm surprised it's allowed.'

'Why ever not,' said Mum. 'Don't you have freedom of religion in America?'

'Ma'am, we have the freest nation on God's earth, but that's not religion. That's superstition.'

We found this a bit hard to swallow after all the rot he'd been talking about swords in stones and ladies in lakes, but Mum gave us a warning glance so we said nothing.

Arthur came in looking pleased with himself and made straight for the hearthrug.

Mr Litterschratter said, 'Hi Arthur, you must be tired out.' Then to Mum. 'Your cat's been following me about all day. I've seen him in just about every place I've been. I didn't know kitties followed people around like dogs do.'

Mum winced at the word kitties. Arthur is no kitty; he's a full-blown grown up tomcat, with duelling scars to prove it.

'Are you sure it was Arthur? The whole town's full of Arthur's relations. Where did you see them all?'

'I'm sure it was Arthur I saw on the cemetery wall. It looked just liked him.'

'Oh that's Mordred. He's always mousing in the graveyard. We think he's Arthur's son as he's very like him. Don't go near Mordred, he's mean. He'll scratch you as soon as look at you.'

'Then I saw Arthur sitting in a shop window; that place with the odd smell and all hung about with crystals and figurines of ladies with holes in the middle.'

'Oh the Green Knight. That would be Gawain. He just sleeps in the window all day. They say he's addicted to the incense.'

'Is he Arthur's son too? I wouldn't know them apart.'

'It's his nephew actually. You can tell it's not Arthur because he has white tips to his ears and Arthur's are totally black. You can't mistake Mordred either if you look closely because his face is thinner and it makes him look really mean. How many more spotted cats did you see?'

'Well I saw one just like Arthur sitting outside the church door. I'm sure he was trying to get inside. Is he another of Arthur's sons?'

'That'd be Galahad,' said Dad decisively. 'We don't know what relation he is but he's always trying to get into the church. He seems to have this thing for sniffing around altar vessels. I don't know why the Vicar puts up with him. You can't mistake Galahad though. Next time you see him try to get him to turn round. He's got a perfect fig leaf just where a gentleman ought to have one.'

Mr Litterschratter looked puzzled.

'He's got a leaf shaped mark on his butt,' said Mum, her American studies coming to the rescue.

Mr Litterschratter blushed, then continued his narrative. 'Then when I strolled up the hill towards the Chalice Well, there was this great big black and white cat sitting on a factory wall. The cat didn't look healthy so I knew it couldn't have been Arthur.'

'A bit moth-eaten, you mean.'

'I'll say. It had lots of bare patches and half an ear missing.'

'If it's the shoe factory that's Kay. It's probably Arthur's half brother though they might be cousins. Kay's the local hero. There were some people came over from Anglesey with this horrible great cat that went around attacking everybody else's cat, so Kay went after it and killed it. I didn't see it myself but people said they heard fighting all night long and in the morning the Anglesey cat was dead. Kay came home ripped to pieces and his people had to spend a fortune on vet bills'

Our guest's eyes were bulging by this time. 'Gee, you sure do have some cats in Glastonbury. But there was this nice little kitty in the abbey grounds. It seemed to be looking for something,' he continued. 'It was very like Arthur but it can't have been him because it was a lot smaller.'

'Oh that's Perceval.' Dad was starting to enjoy the cat saga. 'He's not quite fully-grown yet. I think he's one of Arthur's nephews or he might be a cousin. He lives across the road above the music shop but he's always sniffing around in the Abbey grounds. His owners christened him Perceval but the people in the shop call him Parzifal because it sounds more musical, like the opera. He'll answer to either.'

'Dear me, you do have a lot of Arthur lookalikes.'

'Arthur's people have been here since time immemorial and you know what cats are like, so you'd expect all sorts of sons, cousins, nephews, brothers and half-brothers; and whatever other colours we get, there's always a few like Arthur, spotted black on white with smudged noses.'

'Well I know it really was Arthur who came out to meet me at the top of the lane just now, for he followed me all the way home. He seemed to be limping a little; funny he seems to be all right now.'

Dad leapt out of his chair with a muffled curse and we could hear him thundering up the stairs towards the guest bedroom.

'That wasn't Arthur,' Mum said by way of explanation. 'That was Bedwyr, and Dad's gone racing off upstairs because he's got some very antisocial habits.'

Dad came clumping downstairs clutching another Arthur lookalike, then opened the door and shoved him out very briskly.

'Just caught the beggar in time,' he said. 'It was just about to start digging in the bedclothes.'

'Why'd it want to do that for?' Mr Litterschratter looked as though England was getting beyond his comprehension.

'Because cat's dig holes when they're about to... err... go to the bathroom.' Mum's linguistic skills came to the fore again.

Mr Litterschratter blushed again. We'd heard they are very modest about mentioning lavatories in America.

'We knew who it was when you mentioned the limp. Bedwyr's got a paw missing.'

'How'd he lose it?'

'I don't know. Got it caught in the door trying to get into somebody's bedroom I dare say. He's got a bad reputation for making messes in beds.'

Dad thought he'd better change the conversation before Mr Litterschratter decided he didn't like Somerset. We really needed the money, what with Foot and Mouth coming on top of BSE.

'Would you like to try some real Somerset cider Mr Litterschratter? There's a man just down the road who makes the best cider in the world. I can take you to see where they make it if you like.'

Mum kicked Dad's ankle under the table. It might be the best cider in the world, but the cleanliness of the place leaves something to be desired and she didn't want a super- hygienic American seeing all that went on in there and being put off drinking it.

Dad brought in the glasses and poured our guest a pint straight from the demi-john. Mr Litterschratter took a long swig then gasped.

'Aw, gee. Do you Brits put alcohol in the apple juice?'

'No.' Mum was firm. 'Real English cider is made from apples by fermentation, and alcohol is an integral part of the process. It keeps without any preservatives. It's 100% natural and the process has gone on here in Somerset for hundreds of years.'

Mr Litterschratter took a cautious sip. 'It tastes fine. Do you suppose King Arthur drank cider?'

'I expect so. He was said to be very fond of apples so I'm sure he'd drink cider as well. Would you like some apple pie and cream to finish off with?'

Felix P. viewed the clotted cream with some trepidation. He'd never seen hard cream before, he said. We told him it was a West Country tradition going back to Sir Walter Raleigh's time. We didn't know whether it was or not, just as we didn't know if King Arthur liked apples, but by now we'd all had a bit of cider and were determined to keep our guest happy.

We took our coffee in the sitting room. Mum likes to keep the sitting room for best and we're not allowed in there until we've changed our boots. Mr Litterschratter's shoes were always impeccable, so she said he could go and sit in there any time he liked. He relaxed in the comfortable chair and the conversation turned again to King Arthur.

'What do you make of this story that he's not really dead, then?'

'You mean sitting in a cave under the hill waiting till England needs him?' Dad's mouth started to twitch with suppressed amusement.

'I suppose it could be some sort of suspended animation, you know like the yogis do in the Far East. Anyway, those caves must be very cold and that would slow his metabolic rate right down.'

'Actually, the caves round here are at a constant

temperature of about thirteen degrees. You ought to go and visit Wookey Hole if you like caves. There's been people living in Wookey Hole caves since the Iron Age.'

Mr Litterschratter was not to be diverted from his purpose.

'Yes, but do you think King Arthur could have gotten buried in there some place?'

'No, definitely not.' Mum had had enough of this nonsense and went off to do the dishes.

Dad reached for his pipe and offered our guest his tobacco bowl. He declined, but asked if Dad would mind if he lit a cigar now that there were no ladies present. Dad helped him light up.

'Now I don't think that many people believe King Arthur and his knights are really holed up somewhere waiting to come back. There's been legends like that all over Europe but nobody's ever seen a fossilised king waking up again. But maybe Arthur lives on in spirit; you know, inspiring people who want to be like him.'

'If you mean this reincarnation stuff like the Hindus believe in I won't have it. God's not going to make somebody come back as a cow, or a big black vulture or something. That's sheer heathenish nonsense.'

Dad gulped. How a man could believe in a

children's story of a king being in suspended animation for fifteen hundred years, yet balk at the idea of reincarnation was beyond his comprehension. He looked as if he were about to say so and very forcefully too, when Mum came back in and saved the situation.

'I've often wondered if King Arthur had sons. If he'd lived round here for any length of time then he may have left children. Maybe Arthur lives on in his descendants.'

'But surely Guinevere couldn't have children?'

Mum collected her wits quickly. 'Perhaps it was after Guinvere left him for Lancelot. I couldn't blame him for having had a few lady friends under those circumstances.'

Felix P. looked doubtful. I don't think he liked the idea of his hero having had an extra-marital sex life.

'You know there might be something in this Arthur lives legend if we mean he lives on in his descendants. Maybe there'll be a great leader to come, but of course we won't know he's descended from King Arthur.'

Mum successfully diverted the conversation and talked about other places worth a visit. She wanted to keep our visitor happy because she wanted to keep her guest-room occupied. Dad looked out some guidebooks to the area and helped plan an itinerary for the next few days.

Bath, Wells, Cheddar, Wookey Hole and Bristol; Felix P. Litterschratter did them all. He left at the end of a week, having thoroughly enjoyed himself and given Mum a very large tip. He was off to Cornwall next to see Tintagel, he said. Dad warned him to be careful of the piskies.

'I do hope he gets there before the storm sets in,' Mum said after she'd waved him goodbye. 'There's been an urgent storm warning on the weather forecast. I think we'd better get everything battened down and the livestock in.' We spent the rest of the day making sure nothing could be blown away. We knew what West Country storms could be like.

The storm broke that night and I got up to watch it out of the window. Wham! There goes the thunder. Wow! What a lovely bolt of forked lightning. I loved storms. Mum and Dad slept on. I think you lose a bit of the enchantment when you get older.

There was a long rolling thunderous roar then a flash of lightning that showed trees lashed by a roaring gale, then crash! Something solid sounded as though it was falling to the ground.

I heard a yell from Arthur in the kitchen. That was fighting talk. Then a slamming of the cat flap rudely thrust aside and in the eerie light, I could see Arthur dashing across the yard towards the apple tree. Another flash showed him standing upright on the branch; his head thrown back and his mouth open in a terrible caterwauling screech. I could hear answering yowls from all around as the other local cats galloped to join him.

I flung the window open to listen. There were more feline sounds from the other end of the lane. The building that housed the Cornish Rex must have been struck by lightning and the prisoners set free, because the yelling and screaming almost equalled the howls of anger coming towards us from the town.

The rain poured down, but at each flash of lightning I could see black and white forms racing across the soaking ground to converge around Arthur's tree. Sinister bodies slunk up on them from the other direction. It was an almighty cat fight. After an hour or so I went back to bed but could still hear the growling and snarling till I nodded off.

I awoke next morning to see sun streaming in under the curtains and hear the normal peaceful sounds of the countryside all around me. I looked out of the window and saw the lake, miraculously restored as it always was after a storm. I put on some clothes and joined Dad, pulling on wellies to go and inspect the damage. Thankfully, our buildings were intact and the cows were chewing as placidly as usual. I went out to see the lake. It's always fascinated me, coming up overnight then vanishing again in a day or two.

'Look, over there.' Dad was pointing to a tree floating on the far side of the lake. I plunged in and ran towards it hoping against hope that what I saw wasn't true but alas, it was.

Lying spread-eagled across the twigs was the body of Arthur. I scooped him up and held him but it was too late; he was quite cold and already beginning to stiffen. His coat was ripped in so many places he must have died from loss of blood, but on his face was a look of utter peace. He'd died as he would have wished to die: fighting freakish foreign cats.

We found Bedwyr lying exhausted in the hedge and took him to the vet to be stitched. (His owners were out at work.) The surgery was full of smudge-faced spotted cats in various stages of disrepair. Kay had lost his other ear and Perceval would never be good looking again. We all agreed they'd done a good job and were worth all the vet bills, for piled up in a heap by the side of the lake was the whole army of Cornish Rex; not one of them left alive to pollute our breeding stock of good ratters. And at the bottom of the heap was Mordred: he'd gone over to the other side and died a traitor.

We buried Arthur in the orchard. Dad made him a marker from a nice piece of wood he had left over from something and Mum got out her stencil and wrote *Hic iacet Arthur 2004*. As soon as the paint was dry Dad placed the marker carefully on Arthur's grave, making sure it was neatly lined up with all the other gravestones going off into the distance.

Mum cried a little then and said, 'I shall miss him'.

'We'll all miss him,' said Dad putting his arm around her. 'We'll leave him to rest a couple of weeks before we get another, shall we?'

Mum nodded.

'Then we'll get another Arthur. That red-haired woman from Windmill Hill said she'd got a smudge-nosed spotted kitten in her litter and she was sure it was Arthur's. It'll be ready to leave its mother in about a fortnight.'

'Oh that'll be Isolde.' Mum started to cheer up a little. 'A lovely little cat; grey with white paws. Yes, I fancy one of hers.'

'She said she'd keep it for us.'

Mum smiled, then she kissed him.

'There'll always be an Arthur,' she said.

Deliver Us from Evil.

Wearily, Lindsey pushed her damp hair out of her eyes. The interview room, so nice and sunny in winter was like an oven in August. She didn't think she could stand much more. The sheer wickedness of Gerald Grimes had exhausted her.

There was a tap at the door. She winced, dreading another bout of disturbed malevolence from the next inmate.

'Come in,' she called.

It was the Governor.

'Would you like to join me in my office for tea?' He said. 'It's nice and cool on that side of the building and one of the men on the catering course has produced some nice little cream cakes. He said he'd made them specially for the Vicar.'

'How nice,' she said. 'I suppose I ought to be grateful that somebody's done something positive for once.'

'Oh you mustn't let this place get you down. We do have our successes you know. But who have you been interviewing?'

'Gerry Grimes.'

'What, Grizzly Grimes?' No wonder you look drained. Five minutes of his company is all I can stand. I've been in psychiatric prisons for over twenty years but men like Grizzly still make my blood run cold.

'I suppose I ought to say that he's mentally ill and can't help it.'

'The psychiatrist doesn't think so. He says he's as sane as we are.'

Lindsey shuddered. The thought of such malevolent cruelty being done by someone in sound mind didn't bear thinking about.

'It's his blaming of other people that really gets me. He insists he was sexually abused in the children's home.'

'He might well have been. It's always gone on, but since the media got hold of it every hysteric seeking attention and every petty criminal wanting to get even with those who tried to make him behave throws accusations around. Who did he say did it?'

'He says it was the Bishop of Westchester.'

'That fits. The Bishop's death's been in all the

papers and the telly did a tribute to his life, so who better for a troublemaker to go accusing. I shouldn't take any notice if I were you.'

'He said the Bishop specialised in…' Lindsey hesitated before finding words she felt comfortable using. 'He says he committed brutalities of an intimate nature.'

'How like Grizzly Grimes. "The Bishop showed me how to do it." That's the best excuse I've ever heard.'

The Governor smiled at her. 'I came to say I think you ought to take some leave. You've done very well, and the men seem better behaved since your arrival. But you've got to look after yourself and anyone dealing with Grizzly must need a few days off.'

So Lindsey was on her way to Cornwall. The sun beat down on the car and the road shimmered in the heat. She opened the windows but the traffic noise made her close them again. She realised she had not had a drink for some time. She needed to look for a stopping place but somewhere less frantic than a motorway service station.

Westchester 5 miles, read the sign. The seat of the deceased Bishop; the man known and loved throughout the land as the cuddly television cleric, so appealing, so reassuring, and now subject of a malicious accusation, tempted her curiosity.

She'd stop at Westchester. It would be nice and cool in the cathedral and they'd be sure to have a teashop. She swung the car into the slip road and slowed her speed, the square towers of the cathedral looming ahead of her. She followed the sign for Cathedral Parking and stopped as near to the building as she could, then stepping out into the dazzling sunlight, she walked towards the dark doorway of the great building.

It was cool inside; cool and peaceful. She sat down in one of the pews and looked around her. There was a mass of flowers in one of the alcoves, and a large notice board with letters pinned to it. A memorial to the late Bishop she surmised. She got up to look at it.

On an easel was a framed photograph of the deceased prelate, smiling benignly as usual – or was he smirking? Lindsey cursed the revolting Grizzly Grimes for putting such doubts into her head. The notice board was full of letters from people who said they'd derived great inspiration from his broadcasts.

'…You made me feel so much better…' 'I never believed in God till I saw you on the television…' 'You showed us all how to lead better lives…'

She felt a surge of revulsion. That wasn't pastoral

work. That was self-importance writ large; and a very large fee to go with it. Maybe he wasn't so holy after all. Could Grizzly's accusations possibly have been true? A cold draught seemed to come from behind her.

She turned to go. Out of the corner of her eye she could see a monk in grey habit walking swiftly towards her. Then there was a splintering crash and she felt sharp objects hitting her legs. A large chunk of masonry had hit the floor showering the aisle with fragments. Dabbing at the trickles of blood on her ankles with her handkerchief, she realised that the stone had missed her by inches.

She turned and ran out of the cathedral into the searing sunlight of the close. The ancient walls reflected the sun's rays and she felt as though she were in some sort of gigantic pressure cooker. A notice read *To the Bishop's Garden* and she followed the pointer hoping to find somewhere cool.

The garden shimmered in the heat, the flowers wilting, the rippling stream reflecting stabs of sunlight into her cringing eyes. She screwed them up and looked frantically around for shade. A sign said *Arboretum This Way*. A tree collection: there'd be sure to be shade there.

She dipped her hands in the stream and splashed

her heated face, then walked through the archway to the wooded area. It was cooler there, and silent; no other visitors were in sight. She looked about her and saw great trees, some of them labelled and dated. She was standing beneath a two-hundred-years-old tulip tree, and beside it, a huge weeping birch hung low over the ground like a great tent. She sat on a bench enjoying the shade. How fortunate the Bishop of Westchester had been. She'd love to live in a palace with gardens like this.

Her thoughts returned to the smirking photograph. Perhaps the late Bishop had been driven by ambition and the holiness was just a front. Suddenly she felt cold; so cold she could hardly catch her breath. Coming towards her along the walk was the grey robed monk again. He reached out his hand, and she felt a rush of air as a great branch crashed to the ground beside her. She ran, and didn't stop running till she'd left the cathedral precinct behind her.

She found a pleasant teashop in the new part of town. Spotless in chrome and Formica and bustling with mothers and children, the sheer modernity of the place restored her to her usual sensible self. She was ready to admit now that she must be overtired. She'd never have let Grizzly Grimes upset her composure otherwise. Meeting two falling objects in one afternoon must be coincidence. These old cathedrals were notorious for being short of funds for maintenance, and probably couldn't afford proper gardeners nowadays either. She shouldn't have given in to morbid curiosity and come to Westchester. She'd treat herself to a nice pot of Earl Grey, then continue her journey. She was off duty; on holiday. She'd forget all about work and spend a few days enjoying herself.

Collecting her car, Lindsey drove along the route leading out of town. She averted her eyes as she passed the cathedral. There was no point in upsetting herself again. The sun must have dazzled her for she failed to see the small grey mini that shot out of a gateway ahead of her. There was a screech of metal, the steering wheel lurched out of her hands and the car swerved across the pavement to hit the wall.

Shakily she got out of the damaged vehicle. The grey mini had reversed and driven away, seemingly none the worse. She was sure she'd seen the grey robed figure on the corner, but when she looked again he was gone. A crowd was collecting. She wished they'd all go away.

A traffic warden pushed authoritatively through the milling mob.

'Let me through,' she commanded. 'Did anybody

get his number?'

Apparently no one had. The warden questioned Lindsey and having found her unharmed, checked over the car and said it should be safe enough to drive to the workshop. She directed her to a small garage a few streets away.

The proprietor was kind. He said he'd prepare an estimate at once, and would she like to go with Jason to the office where she could sit and wait.

The youth was awkward, but pleasant enough.

''Oo did it Miss?'

'I don't know. Someone in a grey mini who didn't stop.'

'The only grey mini I know belonged to the Bishop an 'ee's dead.'

'Did you know the Bishop?'

'Of course I knew 'im. 'Ee was the 'ead of governors of the 'ome I was in.'

'Was sort of man was he?' Lindsey couldn't help herself asking.

''Ee was a rotter, but I don't expect you'll believe me wot with 'im being a bishop and me being one of the lads wot was in there.'

'What did he do that was so bad then?'

'Oh wot's the use. You'll never believe me.' The youth turned to go out.

'Come back Jason. I just might believe you.

168

You're not the first person to tell me the Bishop did wrong.'

''Ow do you know the sort of people 'ee'd do wrong with?' Jason looked disbelieving.

'I'm a prison chaplain. People tell me things all the time.'

The young man looked hard at her. 'Grizzly Grimes was it. I 'eard 'ee was inside.'

Lindsey gave an involuntary nod.

'Then you know wot the Bishop did. 'Ee did it to all of us only most of us 'ated 'it and got out of it when we could. I used to volunteer to wash the boss's car or dig the garden so's I wouldn't be in the 'ouse when 'is 'oliness called round.

Lindsey nodded encouragingly, unwilling to do anything to stop the flow.

''Ee'd take us out with 'im in that little old car to somewhere there was nobody around then 'ee'd make us get out and do what 'ee wanted. Sometimes 'ee'd make us go into the garden instead and do it under a big tree that hangs down so's you can't see under it; 'ee even took me to the cathedral once when it was all locked up.'

'Didn't you tell anybody; your teacher perhaps?'

''Oo'd have believed us? We was in there because we was delinquents. Besides, Grizzly would have stuck up for 'im and said it wasn't true.'

'Why would he have done that?'

'Grizzly actually liked it. 'Ee'd be sure to stand where the Bishop would see 'im, then 'ee'd boast about it afterwards. He was really bad was Grizzly. I know the rest of us wasn't much good but Grizzly was rotten through an' through. When I read in the papers what 'ee'd done to all those children I wasn't surprised. The Bishop taught 'im and then 'ee went and did the same to a lot of little kids'

The proprietor came in to report on the car. The youth looked guilty and slipped away.

'Was he bothering you Miss?'

'No, he's a nice lad,' she said.

'He's a bit rough. Been in care and all that, but he loves cars. He'll be a good mechanic when I've finished training him.'

The car would be ready the following afternoon, he continued, and if she needed somewhere to stay he could recommend a guesthouse in a quiet side street.

She thanked him and went out into the fresh air. The sun was setting and though it was still warm, the stifling heat of the day had gone. Following the man's directions, she walked along the main road then turned down a side street that ran along beside the old city wall. The houses were old but soundly maintained – Georgian she thought – though the wall was far older and wide enough for people to walk along the top.

As she rounded a corner she saw the monk again. Hood up and head down, he strode along the wall heading towards the steps that came down just in front of her. She felt a surge of cold again. Suddenly, a large black dog leaped towards her, snarling with dripping jaws. Something pushed her and she fell to the ground. She gasped and shut her eyes as the chill overwhelmed her.

Then somebody was rubbing her hands and speaking reassuringly. She opened her eyes and saw the grey habit. She screamed. A large black cross seemed to descend in front of her and she grabbed at it and held onto it frantically.

'Here, I'll take it off and you can hold it properly.' The voice was educated, though with a trace of a country accent.

She opened her eyes again and saw the monk taking the cord that held the cross from around his neck. He smiled reassuringly.

'I think you're safe now. He's gone.'

Lindsey wasn't sure she ought to trust the monk, though surely he couldn't be evil if he had a cross about him.

He smiled again. 'Let me help you up. You've had two or three narrow squeaks today haven't you.

But I think we know who we're dealing with now. It was the grey mini that gave him away. It was his gimmick you see, he could have had the former bishop's Rolls if he'd wanted but he loved playing the humble cleric.'

Lindsey decided to trust him. With his hood thrown back he looked young; but there was something mature, about those steady grey eyes.

'It was the Bishop, wasn't it? I've been told things about him and presumably he wanted me silenced.'

'You and several others. When you've had an opportunity to collect yourself I'd like you to tell me all you know. If I know why he's not at rest it'll be easier to stop the manifestations.'

'Who are you?' Lindsey said. 'I thought it was you who were after me at first. You were always around when things were happening.'

'I usually am around when things are happening,' said the young man ruefully. 'The Dean called me in to investigate some unpleasant phenomena that have been reported in and around Westchester Cathedral. I'm the Diocesan Exorcist.'

The Bodyguard.

'An aristocrat standing for Parliament in a mining constituency? They'll eat her alive.'

'Or hang her from the nearest lamppost.'

There was a ripple of laughter along the library queue.

'Maybe she ought to get a bodyguard.'

There was more laughter. Titled ladies weren't very popular in the pit villages.

'At least it will wake things up a bit,' said the librarian, stamping the books vigorously and wishing that the council would hurry up and get her a proper electronic scanner. 'Nothing's happened round here since that television crew came making the documentary about the closure of the coal mines.'

There were nods of agreement. Even the death of their Member of Parliament hadn't attracted much interest. Heart attacks were very common at his age.

Then the local party, tired of being dictated to by London, had invited the well-known miners' leader and political maverick Geordie Pityard to represent them in the by-election.

The opposition hit back. They didn't usually bother much in such a safe seat but this time they had a trump card to play. Lady Flora Oldcastle, chat show hostess and Media Personality of the Year had revealed an ambition to go into Parliament, and if anyone could turn that benighted constituency around it was she. "Lady Flora Presents" had the highest television ratings and she'd twice been voted the most popular person in Britain. She couldn't go out without being beset by fans, so getting her out shaking hands with the constituents should be enough to turn the voting around.

Lady Flora arrived poised, beautiful and charming and set about kissing babies, patting dogs and shaking hands with just about everybody. Wherever she went everyone wanted to be in the picture and she was constantly jostled by admirers hoping the cameras were trained in their direction. People took to carrying their own cameras every time they went out in case Lady Flora appeared.

'I'll photograph you if you'll photograph me,' they called to total strangers. The supermarket sold right out of film.

Lady Flora travelled with an entourage. The grave-faced agent and the quietly dressed secretary were always there, but as they never spoke people soon ceased to notice them. It was impossible however, to ignore the striking looking man constantly by her side.

'Is that your boyfriend, Lady Flora?' asked a journalist.

'No, he's my bodyguard.'

The people were duly impressed.

The man was tall, dark and handsome, his athletic good looks providing a magnificent foil for Lady Flora's fair beauty. Several of the girls fell in love with him, though he never gave them any encouragement. It wasn't his looks though, that attracted the most attention, it was the sinister little black case he always carried.

'Do you think he's got a pair of pistols in there?' said a youth.

'Maybe he'd show us if we asked him,' said another.

They asked him but he only smiled.

'You mustn't talk to him when he's on duty,' said Lady Flora firmly, and suitably awed, they never attempted to speak to him again.

'It's not decent, carrying guns around,' was the

opinion expressed in the Workmen's Club. 'Who does he think he is?'

'I don't care who he is, I'm voting the way I've always done.'

Others agreed, but nevertheless Mr Pityard's support was getting thinner. The miners' leader fought hard. He spoke well and he spoke often. He told the people many useful facts. He proposed sensible solutions to some of the country's most pressing problems.

He also fought fair. He never once referred to Lady Flora's grandfather whose mining company had the lowest pay and the highest death rate in the country. He made no mention of her youthful indiscretions with the African archbishop or the Soviet ballet dancer. He said nothing at all about her three divorces or her ex-mother-in-law's missing diamonds. He fought hard but he fought clean.

But clean or dirty you cannot fight the media. A man who promises Utopia tomorrow doesn't stand a chance against somebody famous on the television today. Lady Flora was winning hands down.

Alas, not all of his supporters fought so clean. To be fair to Mr Pityard, the handful of people determined to cause trouble weren't anything to do with him. They weren't even paid up members of the party, they were simply a bunch of ruffians spoiling for a fight.

They didn't dare do much to Lady Flora at first, just a few catcalls and rude gestures. The bodyguard was always with her and though they'd never have admitted it, they were a little afraid of the man who carried the small black case.

Then one Friday night, recently paid and suitably fortified with beer, they decided it was time to do something to show the world what they were made of. Lady Flora was booked to speak in the community centre, her last big meeting before the election.

'Let's gan doon and give her summat to taak aboot.'

'We cannot, she'll have yon bodyguard with her.'

'Then let's get her on the roadside. If she's gone home to titivate she'll be coming in along the back lane. We can hide behind the hedge and hoy stuff at the car then run off afore that bodyguard of hors gets his pistols oot.'

The others thought this a good idea. There was a slight problem of what to do for transport, but it didn't take long to solve. One of the other drinkers had left his car keys on the table and when he went to the gents they simply picked them up on the way out to the car park. The key ring was stamped with the maker's name so it was easy to find the right vehicle.

Having first stopped at a nearby demolition site to pick up urgent supplies, they made their way to a nice twisty bit of road, took up station behind somebody's garden hedge and squatted down out of sight. When they saw Lady Flora's car they waited till it drew level then stood up and hurled lumps of mortar and old rubble at it. There was a clanging of bricks against bodywork and a sound of splintering glass and the driver, unable to see through the shattered windscreen veered off the road into the ditch.

The television van, which had been following Lady Flora all day, arrived on the scene and screeched to a halt. The camera crew leapt out and at the sight of three large men holding something black and sinister in their hands the assailants fled, but not before their faces were captured on film.

So, unfortunately, was Lady Flora's. The media men didn't recognise her at first. The plain-faced woman with short mousy hair who scrambled out of the ditch bore no resemblance to the beautiful blonde goddess the public adored.

It was her voice that gave her away. There was no mistaking that ice-cold bell-like accent. Unmistakable too was the string of expletives she uttered and the unfavourable opinion she expressed of all of the inhabitants of the constituency she hoped to represent. The television crew recorded it all.

The bodyguard recovered first. He scrambled around in the wreckage and emerged clutching his little black case and what appeared to be a blonde wig. Lady Flora gave a strangled howl and tried to snatch away the camera.

'Quick, inside,' said her protector, taking her arm firmly and propelling her through the gate in the hedge.

'Lady Flora's been in an accident,' he said to the housewife standing in the doorway. 'She needs to tidy up, she's got a meeting in a few minutes. Where's the bathroom?'

The woman nodded silently and pointed. The bodyguard pushed his charge in then went in after her.

'Here, you can't go into the bathroom with a lady,' the householder called after him, shocked.

'Don't be silly. I'm her beautician,' he snapped.

The television crew recorded that too.

Lady Flora emerged after a short interval as poised and beautiful as ever. Only a few minutes late, she charmed the audience as she gave the last speech of her campaign. She was wonderful. Everybody loved her.

Then they got home and turned on the news and there, safe on their own sofas out of reach of her charms, they saw that their idol was false. Plain, blotchy-faced and virtually without eyelashes, she wore a *wig* for goodness sake! And whoever had heard of a boy beautician?

But worse of all was the language. It wasn't that she swore that annoyed them, they didn't really blame her for that; they'd have done it themselves in the circumstances. It was what she said about the constituents that really incensed them and it all sounded so much worse with the expletives replaced by beeps.

'*Beep* miners! *Beep Beep* ignorant *Beep*! Those *Beep* can go and *Beep* their *Beep* election! I've had as much of the *Beep* to last me a *Beep* lifetime! *Beep!*'

The library queue was in full cry the following morning.

'Stuck up so-and-so, who does she think she is.'

'Coming here playing Lady Muck.'

'Thinks she can call us what she likes just because her dad's an earl'.

Village politics had returned to normal.

'Boo,' they called next time Lady Flora stopped off to woo the crowds in the shopping centre. 'Gan Hyem,' they shouted when she alighted from her

Rolls Royce to seek admiration from the men queuing up outside the jobcentre. 'We don't think titled ladies belong here,' said the mothers waiting to collect their children from school.

She lost. She lost the election and she lost her deposit. She had the lowest vote of any candidate who had ever stood for Parliament in that constituency. Mr Pityard was elected with a massive majority to become yet another thorn in the flesh of his parliamentary party.

The new MP's efforts to bring back work to his constituency were not successful: the government just wasn't interested in reopening the coalmines. However, the publicity arising from the by-election did a lot of good in other ways.

A famous producer looking for a suitably deprived background for his latest film thought that the streets he'd seen on the television coverage of the by-election would be just right to convey the atmosphere he wanted. The production crew moved in and many local people became film extras.

It was a phenomenal success. "Betty Errington", the heart-warming tale of a redundant miner's daughter struggling against the odds to become a famous atomic scientist, won seven Oscars. The village was in the news again and this time the fame lasted.

Because of the world-wide interest occasioned by the film, the North East Redevelopment Department (NERD) was given a European grant to revitalise the area. They erected a big sign, "Betty Errington Country" on the A19 and built a film studio on the site of the old pit yard. A special effects workshop and a theatrical costumier followed, and in the fullness of time, a drama school and college for scriptwriters. Employment boomed: so did the pubs.

Lady Flora's popularity never recovered and her ratings dropped. Viewers aren't stupid; they don't like television personalities who pretend to like them then say rude things about them when they think they aren't listening. Before long she found herself out of work along with the rest of her entourage.

This didn't bother her beautician. He set up a gymnasium and beauty parlour just up the road from the new studios. He is making a fortune out of all the young people who want to become film stars and his salon is as popular with the young men as it is with the women. It's the sign above the door that pulls the boys in. He's called his establishment "Bodyguard."

Getting Rid of Charlie.

I knew I'd have to get rid of Charlie. He'd become superfluous. There was so much more I wanted to do with my life. I'd long since ceased to care for him and I couldn't remember why I ever did. I was sure he didn't love me either, though he could be quite affectionate when he wanted something.

I'd enrolled in an assertiveness class. 'Take charge of your life,' the tutor had said. 'You don't have to live up to anybody else's expectations. Give up anything that isn't any use to you any more.'

Charlie wasn't any use to me or to anyone else as far as I could see. All he did was eat and sleep. Sometimes he couldn't even be bothered to greet me when I came home from work. I'd be much better off without him.

As I turned the key in the lock I knew exactly

where he'd be, and sure enough there he was stretched out on the sofa with his mouth wide open, snoring. I longed to hit him, but of course I didn't. I tiptoed past him to the kitchen to make myself a snack but as soon as he heard the fridge door open he woke up and started demanding something for himself as usual. I knew then, as I served up his dinner onto his plate, that if I was to have any independence at all Charlie would have to go.

But how was I to get rid of him? He'd never go of his own accord; he was far too comfortable here. Besides, I was pretty sure nobody else would have had him. I thought I'd got rid of him once before, when he took a fancy to that blonde woman a couple of streets away, but she soon got sick of him and threw him out. He'd come back to me with his tail between his legs looking very sorry for himself and I'd taken pity on him and let him stay. He seemed grateful, and was utterly charming for a few days, but he soon lapsed back into his fat lazy habits again.

As the weeks went by and I became more and more assertive, it slowly dawned on me that the only way I was going to get rid of Charlie was to kill him. I repressed the thought at first because it made me feel guilty, but as time went on and I became more and more determined to make something of myself, I knew that with Charlie around I'd never become mistress of my own life . Why, even though it was my wages that had paid for it, I couldn't even sit on my own sofa!

The idea of bumping him off gradually grew on me, but it was surprisingly difficult to think of a way of doing it without alerting his suspicions. He was quite intelligent underneath all that lazy fat and could be very observant when it suited him. The very sight of him just lying there snoring made me want to strangle him while he slept but I knew that wouldn't work because he'd just wake up and go for me.

The alternatives weren't so easy either. Have *you* ever worked out how you'd kill somebody? I thought of getting him drunk and drowning him in the bath, but I could never get him to take enough alcohol. He just wasn't keen on it. Then there was that nasty case in the papers where a woman locked her husband in the garden shed and set fire to it. Charlie liked going down the shed. Maybe next time he was in there I could slink up and ignite it before he'd noticed the smell of petrol. But what if the neighbours heard him yelling? Besides, when I thought about it, I just couldn't bring myself to burn him alive. Even old fat slob Charlie didn't deserve such a horrible end. Anyway, I needed the shed for the gardening tools.

I went to the library to seek inspiration. Real-life crime wasn't much help; apparently there aren't any undetectable poisons. Poisons in general aren't very easy to come by nowadays, direct access to things like arsenic and strychnine went out when Agatha Christie was a girl.

Crime fiction wasn't much use either. It was all too far-fetched. Inject him with an air embolism? He'd wake up as soon as he felt the syringe going in. Tie a brick round his ankles and throw him in the river? All by myself? I'd need at least a couple of helpers. Take him up a mountain and wait for him to die of altitude sickness? Really, how silly can you get!

There was, however, a poster on the library wall telling mums and dads to be careful to lock up dangerous substances away from children. That gave me the idea. Maybe I should look for some common house or garden poison and kill him with that, then if anybody ever found out it would be easy to pass it off as an accident.

I went to the do-it-yourself shop to see what I could find. Sure enough there were lots of items on the shelves labelled "poison". The place was fairly bristling with dangerous substances. The obvious choice seemed to be slug pellets; the carton being liberally splattered with awful warnings. I duly bought a supply of these delicacies, carefully prepared Charlie's favourite dish (making sure the gravy was dark enough to disguise the blue colour) and then stirred in a handful. Charlie wasn't fooled. He took one bite, then favouring me with the withering glance he always gave me when he didn't like my catering, pushed his plate aside and went back to his sofa (my sofa!) and fell asleep.

I went back to the do-it-yourself store next weekend for further inspiration. Unfortunately all the other poisons were strongly-scented things like turpentine, bleach, disinfectant and paint thinner and I just couldn't imagine Charlie not noticing if I added them to his dinner.

Back to the library for more true crime. Still no help for the wicked. How do you push somebody out of the car without being seen by other drivers? How can you shove somebody over a cliff when he's too darn lazy to go for a walk with you? A knife? The books all said that over half the victims of stabbing attacks lived to tell the tale. And I'd have all that blood to clean up afterwards.

I looked up suicide next. People seemed to be more successful with that, and the most popular method was drug overdose. Well that should be easy enough. I'd see the doctor, tell him I couldn't sleep and get him to prescribe me some sleeping tablets. It didn't work. After giving me a thorough examination he said there was nothing wrong with me, and I'd sleep all right if I took more exercise. I even thought of using aspirins but even one aspirin tastes so horrible there's no way I could have slipped a lethal dose into Charlie's food without his noticing.

In the end it was the local paper that gave me the answer. "Youth gets Ten Years for Manslaughter", said the headline. The article went on to say that a teenage mugger tried to knock an old lady out in order to steal her handbag. He hit her over the head with a brick, but unfortunately he hit her too hard and she died. Simple. Why ever didn't I think of that before.

Killing Charlie with a brick should be easy. There were plenty of bricks at No. 27 where they were building a garage. As soon as it was dark I borrowed a brick from the pile and hid it under the hedge. Next time I came in from work I looked through the window to make sure Charlie was asleep, slipped the brick into my bag, opened the door quietly and tiptoed into the living room. Charlie woke up and stared me right in the face. I couldn't do it. I left the brick where it was and gave him his dinner.

It took me several days to pluck up courage to try it again. Twice I slipped the brick into my bag and planned to do the deed and each time Charlie woke up just as I was coming into the room and I lost my nerve.

Then one evening as I was getting ready to leave the office, the boss came in and started to criticise a piece of work I'd done and insisted that I do it again. I'd just finished it when he decided he wanted it done yet another way. Fuming, I stayed on till I'd done it again and was over an hour late getting home. By the time I'd been elbowed aside on the platform and trampled on inside the underground I'd had enough of males to last me a lifetime. Charlie was definitely going to meet his end tonight.

I tiptoed up the drive and peeped through the window. There he was, fast asleep on the sofa as usual. I picked up the brick, slipped off my shoes, and slunk around to the back door. It opened silently — I'd oiled it a few days before. Creeping up the passage and holding my breath, I carefully pulled the living room door open. Then with a yell of glee I pounced, and he only had time for one last startled glance before I hit him.

There was nothing to it really, just a couple of wallops and he was gone. It was a pity about the nosebleed, I had to wash the cushion-cover afterwards.

I picked him up and put him in a dustbin liner, tucked it under my arm, got into the car and drove to the tip.

'Good riddance you useless old cat,' I said as I threw him into the skip, hurling his litter tray and his feeding dishes after him. I sang light-heartedly to myself as I drove home, well on the way to freedom at last.

Now all I had to do was get rid of Alec....

A Matter of Conscience.

We had always known that our cat was not like other cats. She looked different. Her coat was cocoa brown and she had deep violet eyes; and wasn't that head of hers just a little bit larger than usual?

'I've never seen a cat like that before,' said the Cat Lady to whom we reported finding her. 'Perhaps she's one of these new breeds they're always inventing. You'd think her owners would have come forward to claim her, she must be quite valuable,' she said.

'Look. Do you think you could look after her for a few days, just till we find out whom she belongs to? We're up to the eyes at the moment.' She looked harassed.

We agreed to look after her and the cat stayed, and as nobody ever found out where she'd come from eventually everyone agreed she was ours. Everyone agreed too, that she was a most unusual cat.

It was her fastidiousness we noticed next; she insisted in eating her meals at the table. We weren't having that of course; but when we tried putting her dish on the floor she gave a disgusted look and walked out through the cat-flap, her tail held high in indignation. We compromised by giving her her meals on the scullery table, though we had to be careful to wipe it down and dry it first. She wouldn't touch tinned cat food and she wouldn't eat raw meat. Eventually we just gave her a helping of whatever we were having and she seemed to enjoy that, though she didn't always finish her vegetables.

She ignored the litter tray we put down for her so we assumed she was using the garden, till one day Jim saw her ducking under the door of the outside lavatory and realised who it was who'd been using it. We didn't use it much ourselves, and to be honest we'd been blaming each other for not pulling the flush.

Jim found an old piece of chain and lengthened the pull. 'If you use our loo you'll jolly well pull the chain after you!' He said, looking her sternly in the eye.

She stared back unblinkingly. A few hours later

we heard someone using the flush. She always flushed the lavatory after that and before long we'd ceased to find it unusual.

Then there was the matter of beds. We'd made her a nice bed in a cardboard box in the scullery, but she wouldn't have it. She insisted on sleeping on the bed in the spare room. We disagreed, but in the end we let her sleep on an old towel we put over the bedspread. She accepted this, but insisted on regular changes of linen by dragging the towel off the bed every few days and dumping it beside the laundry basket. After that we just changed it when we did the laundry, and if we forgot, she'd help herself to a clean towel from the airing cupboard. She never had any trouble in opening doors.

She liked watching television, especially the news and world affairs. We had an old push button set then and she soon learnt to switch it on and hunt around for something that interested her. Wars, dictators and presidential elections were her favourite topics, though she enjoyed an occasional cartoon, especially if it had a cat in it. We were getting a lot of interference with our television programmes around that time and oddly enough, the cat seemed to know in advance when reception was going to be bad; for she was never watching the television when it happened. We got to be able to predict it too after a while, just by watching the cat. If we saw her going up the hill towards the quarry, presumably to worry the wildlife, we knew that the television would go haywire about twenty minutes afterwards.

The recent doings at the quarry were a great source of resentment in the neighbourhood. The quarry had been long disused and was a popular site for bird-watching. Then an engineering company rumoured to have defence contracts with unpleasant regimes, bought it and put up some buildings for their experimental work. They erected a huge fence with notices saying, "KEEP OUT", and made sure that the bird-watchers had nowhere to peep their binoculars through. We were all sure that the interference with our television programmes was something to do with the work being done at the quarry. There were several attempts to have it closed down, but nothing ever came of them.

The local cats loved the quarry. There were plenty of birds and plenty of cover for hunting them and the fence was no problem for a cat. Our cat often went there, but we suspected that she only went when she couldn't watch television, because she never went there when the reception was good.

'How on earth does she know?' I said.

Jim grinned. 'Maybe she's found out what's

going on at the quarry. What a pity she can't talk. If we could prove the interference was coming from up there we'd be able to go to the council and get it stopped!'

We knew she couldn't talk but after a while we began to suspect that she could understand what we were saying. Oh, I know what you're thinking; people think their pets understand every word they say, when all they're doing is looking pleased someone's paying attention to them. But our cat really did seem to understand what we were saying to each other. How else could she have known we were planning to take her to the vet? The Cat Lady had made us promise to have the cat spayed, but every time we phoned the vet to make an appointment she disappeared, so after several attempts we gave up. We thought she might have been spayed already, for at first she showed no interest in other cats and the local moggies seemed rather in awe of her and tended to avoid her.

Till the day the boys came round!

If you've never suffered from a visitation of tom-cats, think yourselves lucky. Those tom-cats were revolting: they screeched, they howled, they fought, they clawed great lumps of flesh off each other and they stank. One big ginger tom was particularly obnoxious. Jim threw numerous buckets of water at it but it just kept coming back to howl and stink some more. Our cat took no notice of them. She simply stayed at home and refused to have anything to do with them.

Then one day when I went out and forgot to close the window, I returned to find Big Ginger slinking out through it. The living-room smelt a bit but as our cat just sat there looking smug we thought that maybe nothing had happened.

But it had happened. Before long the cat was visibly pregnant. We didn't dare tell the Cat Lady, so we borrowed a book from the library and prepared to make a decent job of bringing up the kittens. The cat seemed happy enough and she still went up to the quarry regularly to hunt.

Then one night we heard scrabbling noises from the landing and found her getting herself a clean towel from the airing cupboard. We put several clean towels on the bed for her. She nodded her thanks then indicated that she would like to be left alone. An hour later she called out to us and she proudly displayed a minute kitten for our admiration.

She called her daughter Mreee. Mreee grew rapidly. Her eyes were deep violet like her mother's and she had her mother's rich cocoa brown fur, though there was a hint of a ginger stripe in it. She seemed to have inherited some of her mother's intelligence too, for by the time she was a month old, she was scrambling onto the lavatory unaided – though she fell in a few times and had to be rescued.

Her mother never left her during the first month, so she never visited the quarry. There didn't seem to be any interference with the television any more and we'd often come in to find the two of them sitting watching the news. When Mreee could eat solids, her mother would occasionally go out and leave her for us to look after, though she was never out for long. She wasn't out long enough to have visited the quarry and perhaps her interest in it had evaporated now that she could enjoy her television programmes without interruption.

Then the strangest thing happened. One afternoon, an oval object looking very like an old-fashioned bathtub with four feet, landed in the garden. The neighbours said afterwards it must have been something to do with the quarry and we didn't enlighten them. Nobody would have believed us if we had. We were never certain that we really believed it ourselves.

It happened very suddenly. There was a whooshing noise; the cat gave a startled cry and stared out of the window. I looked up and saw the bathtub thing hovering over the lawn about to land.

'What the...' said Jim as the cat grabbed Mreee by the scruff and pushed her hastily behind the cushion on his chair. She gave us an imploring look as though asking us not to divulge her hiding place, just as three cats marched in through the cat-flap and surrounded her. Each cat looked exactly like ours except that it wore a leather strap diagonally from one shoulder across the chest to the waist and each strap bore a metal cylinder. Then they encircled her so that every cylinder pointed directly at our cat.

She stood up straight, as though she were standing to attention, while the cat who seemed to be in charge stood in front of her spitting and snarling. She remained silent and dignified when the two lesser cats took up position behind her; and she did not look back as they marched her off through the cat-flap. We were too flabbergasted to do anything but sit and watch helplessly, and by the time we'd collected our wits again they had all entered the bathtub, taken off and flown away.

We couldn't tell anybody where the cat had gone for nobody would have believed us. We certainly didn't tell the Cat Lady when she made her annual call. We didn't tell her about the kitten either, for we were supposed to have had our cat neutered. We just told her that the cat had gone, and no, we didn't want another one just yet.

We brought up Mreee as our own for we felt that her mother would have expected it and we were sure her mother would come back for her one day. Mreee grew up to be charming and beautiful, and really quite intelligent for a cat, though not of course, as intelligent as her mother.

We did however, take Mreee to be spayed. We agonised over this. We felt bad about it afterwards. We were certain her mother wouldn't have approved. But we did it because we knew we must. Well wouldn't you have done the same if you were in charge of a human baby whose father was a gorilla?

The Worm Turns.

'Curiouser and curiouser,' said Jenny. She could have sworn she had seen something grinning at her from the compost heap, but when she had blinked it had gone.

She shook her head bemusedly. It was a very hot day and she knew that the heat distorted things. 'I'm letting that heap get on my nerves,' she said to herself.

There was definitely something odd about it. Everything was rotting down far too quickly: the grass cuttings she'd put there only yesterday were gone already. Jenny didn't like things she couldn't understand. She mentioned her unease to Pete but he poo-pooed it as usual – he was always a bit arch about her lack of scientific education.

'I expect it's something to do with that stuff Alec

gave me. He said it would make the compost rot down faster.'

Alec was Pete's brother who worked at the agricultural research station. Jenny didn't like him. Supercilious and snide, he'd come around for a free meal, get drunk on Pete's home-made beer, then start belittling Jenny. He was careless with his work too, and would boast about all the clever short cuts he'd made. He didn't seem to care that he might be putting several months' research at risk.

Jenny said no more about the heap but she took to avoiding it as much as she could. She threw the grass clippings onto it from a distance and she buried the cat's victims with the spade instead of just kicking soil over them. Maybe she had imagined that sharp-toothed grin, but she wasn't taking any chances.

As the summer wore on a strange plant began to grow out of the heap. It had a long tendril, just like a vine. Pete said it must be a squash, self-sown from the seed of one of the fancy varieties Alec had brought them to try. They had great long stems didn't they? But Jenny wasn't convinced. The plant had no leaves. An experienced gardener, she knew that all plants had to germinate seed-leaves before they could develop anything else.

'Just a vine of some sort,' said Alec curtly when

she showed it to him, and disappeared indoors to sample some of Pete's home brew before Jenny could argue.

The vine grew rapidly. The stem became fat and rope-like and developed an unpleasant bronze sheen, but it still didn't have any leaves. It had a nasty smell too sometimes, especially after she'd given the heap a dead bird. Jenny wanted to dig it out and burn it but Pete wouldn't let her.

'I want to see what it turns into,' he said.

'I don't. I'm sure I've seen it move.'

'Nonsense! How could it? You've got far too vivid an imagination.'

Jenny didn't confide in Pete again. She didn't even tell Pete when the vine made a grab at her ankle when she was putting the washing out. Fortunately the grass was still damp so she was wearing her wellingtons. The thing didn't seem to like rubber for it let go immediately. She wore her wellingtons every time she went into the garden after that and it never bothered her again, though she often saw it trying to sneak up on the birds.

Assuming it didn't like the taste of rubber, she tried an experiment. She threw an old rubber glove onto the heap and watched for a few minutes. Nothing happened. Next time she went down the garden however, the glove was lying in the middle of the lawn. Curious. She supposed the cat could have played with it but she didn't think so; the cat seldom went into that part of the garden now. The birds seemed to be avoiding it too, even when she was digging and exposing a lot of grubs for them. Odder and odder.

Then one day when they were working together in the garden, the creature made a grab at Pete's ankle. He fell over with a curse and Jenny quickly took her spade and chopped off the end of the tendril. The vine writhed angrily and she was sure she heard a sound like gnashing teeth.

'Now do believe me?' Jenny demanded as she helped him to his feet. 'I told you that thing could move!'

'Nonsense. I just tripped over it. Don't be neurotic.'

Jenny didn't have time to worry about the strange plant during the next few days because the cat went missing and she was kept busy ringing around the animal welfare organisations, posting advertisements, and checking the hedges and ditches for dead or injured cats. She never found her.

'Something must have eaten it,' said Pete.

Jenny began to suspect that something might indeed have eaten it. She'd have liked to confide her fears to Pete but she didn't. He'd never have believed her and he'd only insult her intelligence again.

It wasn't until the creature whipped Sue's bikini top off that Pete took it seriously. Jenny didn't care much for Pete's sister, whose idea of coming to stay was to lie in the sun until somebody called her in for meals. But when Sue ran in clutching her bare bosom and screaming that some octopus thing had tried to grab her, Jenny almost liked her. Pete would have to listen to her concerns now.

'Why didn't you tell me?' He said maddeningly, when Jenny repeated all that she had seen the vine do in the last few weeks.

He researched the vine creature with scientific thoroughness. When Jenny told him it didn't like rubber he borrowed her wellingtons to protect himself, then took her rubber gloves and pushed them into the heap with the spade. Next time they went down the garden the gloves were lying on the lawn. Pete tried it again with a bit of old tyre, with the same result. Then, having been told of its fondness for raw meat, he took one of the pork chops intended for dinner, held it out on the spade and offered it to the vine. It ignored him: maybe it didn't like being watched. Pete left the chop on the grass and came in for his dinner (Jenny had to make do with an egg) and when they came out again the chop had gone and the nasty smell was hanging about the heap again.

Pete tried several more experiments over the next few days, but he could never catch the creature in the act. It seemed to have become shy of performing in public.

Then the people next door went on holiday, gave Jenny and Pete the key and asked them to look after the house. This gave Pete the opportunity he needed. He could watch the garden from next-door's bedroom window while Jenny presented the vine with some meat. It worked! As soon as Jenny was out of sight the tendril whipped out, grabbed the bait, then drew it under the compost.

They repeated the experiment several times and the creature always took the bait. Sometimes Pete caught a glimpse of the grinning teeth too. He particularly enjoyed those teeth. Then one evening he saw something he didn't enjoy at all, and it quite put him off scientific experimentation for some time. One of their neighbours had an elderly dog with a fondness for trespassing. It scrambled through the hedge one day and ran into the garden sniffing eagerly. Before it could say 'Woof,' the vine thing had grasped it round the neck and dragged it into the heap. The heap twitched a little, then lay still.

'Jenny, it's eaten the spaniel,' said Pete, rushing into the house. He looked sick.

'I saw it kill that old dog. It came into the garden to have a sniff around and the vine thing just grabbed it and pulled it into the heap.' Pete put his head between his hands and groaned.

Jenny was firm. 'That thing has got to be killed.'

'How?'

'Weedkiller, I suppose. Give it some of that stuff you use on the path.'

Pete stuffed a chicken with weedkiller and presented it to the vine. It loved it. It loved all the other makes of weedkiller too. It grew bigger and glossier and the smell became even worse.

'Maybe it isn't a plant. Perhaps we should try slug-pellets.'

It thrived on slug-pellets. It thrived on all known insecticides, disinfectants, rat poison, mothballs, aspirins, anti-dandruff shampoo; even the stuff Pete had been prescribed for his acne. It grew even larger.

'We'll have to get help,' said Jenny firmly.

'Where from? The police would never believe us.'

This was true; Pete had once reported a neighbour for receiving stolen goods, only to find the man running a perfectly legitimate junk stall at the boot fairs.

'Isn't there a government department to do with agriculture or something?' said Jenny. 'They're supposed to know all about pests and diseases.'

'Agriculture! Of course! I'll ask Alec. He's in agricultural research. I'll ask him over to dinner and tell him then.'

Jenny rebelled. She'd had enough of Alec. It was probably his fault they had the thing in the compost heap in the first place for he'd taken that special compost accelerator from work. She'd always been taught that taking things from work was stealing, and surely it wasn't safe trying out something they hadn't finished researching yet?

And Pete should have consulted her before inviting Alec over to dinner. He'd emptied the freezer with his experiments and spent all her housekeeping money on the weedkillers and pesticides. They would have to make do with egg and chips and that smart Alec would be sure to say something snide about the catering, especially when he'd had a few.

Well there'd be no drinking in her house tonight; she'd make sure of that! She put on her wellingtons, emptied all of Pete's home-brew into the bucket, stamped off down the garden then threw all the horrid stuff onto the compost heap. Then she took up her spade and dug angrily in the border; they would jolly well have dinner when she felt like it making it and not before.

So angry was she that she didn't notice anything stirring in the heap until something brushed against her leg. She kicked it impatiently, then started back in alarm. The vine plant had left the compost heap and was rolling crazily across the lawn, and attached to its thick end was a huge, brown, leathery thing, like an outsize potato, with three big eyes and a great gash of a mouth outlined with spiky teeth.

It seemed to be in some sort of distress for its eyes rolled alarmingly and its head, if that's what it was, gave a series of little jerks and shudders.

'Pete! Pete!' she called. She held the spade defensively in front of her.

'What on earth's the matter with... Hell!' He cried, as he saw the thing lurching towards him.

The tentacle swung out to grab him. It missed. The creature lurched unsteadily towards him again, then gave a great 'Hic!' and rolled over squirming helplessly.

'Why, I do believe it's drunk,' said Jenny laughing. It must have liked Pete's home brew. 'Here Pete, hold the spade. I think I know what to do with it now.'

She ran indoors to fetch Pete's bottle of whisky, then despite Pete's protestations, she put her foot down firmly on the tendril and emptied the bottle into that great gaping mouth.

The horrible teeth gnashed. Would it reject the whisky? It did not. It loved it and sucked it down in great gurgling gulps; then rolled over and lay still.

Pete wanted to wait till Alec arrived before disposing of it but Jenny was having none of it; the thing might be even nastier with a hangover. She lifted her spade and chopped the tendril into little pieces, then did the same to its head. The fragments writhed a little, then lay still. When she was certain they had stopped moving she put them into the incinerator and burnt them.

'We can't risk it propagating from cuttings,' said Jenny firmly.

Pete never did tell Alec about the thing in the compost heap. He didn't need to now and he wasn't sure Alec would have believed him. Jenny wanted to incinerate the compost too but Pete said it wasn't necessary; he'd riddled it and there was definitely nothing in it. It was the best compost they'd ever had and he needed it for the genetically modified sundews Alec had given him. He was going to plant them in the greenhouse and watch them trapping all the insects.

The compost certainly suited the sundews. They grew tall and lush and there wasn't a whitefly in the greenhouse that year. Pete spent most of his time watching them these days, though he'd always come out fast when a meal was in the offing.

How odd that she'd had to call him three times today. It wasn't like Pete to be late for his dinner. Funny, he didn't seem to be in the greenhouse either.

Where on earth could he have got to?

And Did Those Feet.

'Come along scar-face. Get that donkey loaded. The Romans won't want to see the likes of you after nightfall.'

Aemon sighed as he heaved the heavy sacks onto the donkey's back. Though they often laughed at his withered arm, neither his uncle nor his cousins ever offered to help him load the beast. He wished he didn't have to live with them but he had nowhere else to go. The fire that had killed his family and crippled him had burnt his parents' house down and all he had left in the world was his donkey.

His uncle had been pleased to see the donkey. 'We can use it to carry the lead,' he'd said. 'Your cousins and I are far too busy mining it to transport the stuff too. Now we've got our own donkey we can concentrate on working where the real money is.'

He'd promised Aemon his keep, though it was grudging. His uncle's family were well shod but Aemon went barefoot, and when he said he had no winter clothes his aunt had given him a stained, tattered old cloak of his uncle's that was too worn to mend.

He'd been given a bed with his male cousins but as soon as he'd managed to repair the lean-to for his donkey he slept there to get away from the constant taunting. 'Old one-eye,' they called him, or 'wingy,' referring to his useless arm, which had contracted to the shape of a chicken's wing.

He'd soon got used to seeing with one eye, but learning to cope one-handed took a lot longer. Determined to succeed, he'd found he could swing a sack up onto the donkey's back unaided, but tying the ropes had been a problem until he discovered that he could do it holding one end with his teeth.

As soon as he could find a way to earn his own living he'd get away from his unpleasant relations. His father had traded lead with the Romans: maybe he could revive the old mine when he was stronger. He'd use this opportunity of visiting the Roman camp to practise his Latin.

'You're to give the sacks to a man named Josephus and make sure he gives you the right money,' his uncle said. 'He called here this morning to buy flour, but we didn't have enough. Your aunt and the girls have been busy grinding it all day. Hurry back before dark; they say there's been thieves about and I want to bar the gates early.'

Aemon didn't mind visiting the Romans' encampment; they often tipped well. It was just that he hadn't seen Mara lately and he'd promised to take her some firewood. He'd call out to her as he passed and she'd understand.

Mara had saved his life. She had seen the fire and dragged his unconscious body clear of the flames, then taken him to her hut and nursed him till he could get around again. He'd helped her as much as he could. Widowed with young children, she needed to work to support herself and she'd been grateful when Aemon could watch the children while she tended her vegetable plot.

As soon as he could walk, he'd minded the children while she went out helping the other women of the village. She'd weave, sew and grind corn in return for a basket of food and would earn a few coins occasionally by looking after children for mothers in childbed. She didn't want Aemon to go foraging for wood at first; his arm still had not healed, but he said he was better for the fresh air and anyway, the donkey needed the exercise. He stayed with Mara all summer, but knew he'd have to go before winter set in. Living off her slender stores he knew she couldn't afford to feed him as well as her children.

It was a bright autumn afternoon and the sun slanted down among the rich reds and golds of the foliage. Aemon hummed to himself as he jogged along, the donkey trotting contentedly beside him. It was a good little beast and would work well if properly fed. He felt a twinge of resentment against his aunt when he remembered that she'd take handfuls of the hay he'd made for winter to help start the fire in the mornings. As soon as winter was over, he'd try to get enough trade transporting goods to keep himself and maybe help Mara a little too.

Mara would look after him. She'd wanted him to stay; his mother had been kind to her when her husband died, she'd said. He could teach the biggest boy to build, then between them they could add another room to the house, and show the younger ones how to fish and set snares. He .might be crippled and scarred but he could still show them how to do a man's work.

Mara's house was on the edge of the village and she called a greeting as he passed. The children ran out asking him to stay but their mother, seeing the sacks the donkey was carrying, called them back.

'Aemon will come and see us another day,' she said.

The Romans' camp was some distance away and he could see the smoke from their campfire at the foot of the Tor. The donkey trotted forward briskly, its keen nose smelling the fire. A wise little beast, it knew that camps usually meant unloading of burdens and if it was lucky, a handful of something tasty to eat too.

As soon as he saw the men, Aemon knew that these people weren't Romans. Their tunics reached almost to the ground and they had brightly coloured cloths tied around their heads. The Roman Empire was wide: these people must be from one of the eastern provinces.

A tall man came forward to greet him. He smiled at the youth and waved to one of his men to come and unload the donkey.

'Are you Josephus, Sir?'

'I am he.'

Josephus spoke Latin slowly and listened patiently to Aemon's halting sentences, then asked; 'Would you like a drink of wine before you leave?'

Aemon thanked him but said he'd better not tarry. He wanted to be home before dark; he'd heard there were outlaws around. The man patted the donkey, thanked Aemon gravely for his services and gave him a couple of coins for himself.

Aemon examined the coins when he was well clear of the camp. Josephus had been generous. There was enough in his pouch now to pay Mara to make a winter cloak for him. She'd offered to make him one when she saw the tattered old wrap his uncle had given him but he'd refused. He knew she could earn a useful sum weaving for one of the wealthy families instead. Now he could accept her offer and repay her properly. Tired now, he hauled himself up onto the donkey's back and let it walk for a while.

Suddenly, the donkey stopped, snorting at something in the bushes. Aemon glanced around him in alarm: he knew he couldn't defend himself from attackers. But the donkey didn't seem to be afraid. It lowered its head and nuzzled at something in the undergrowth at the side of the track. Aemon slid off its back and keeping a firm hold on the bridle, bent down to look, then started back in surprise. He could see a bare foot protruding from under a low-growing shrub.

The foot twitched and the owner, whoever it was uttered a groan.

'Who are you, are you injured?' Aemon called.

There was no reply. Aemon went down on one knee to look under the leaves and was shocked to see the naked body of a youth of about his own age. Hastily, using his good hand and his teeth, he tied the donkey's bridle to a sapling and crawled down under the bush to see what was the matter.

The youth lay in a crumpled heap. There was blood about his head and more around his chest, though that could have been from the bloodied nose.

Aemon took one of the lad's hands into his and spoke gently to him.

'Can you hear me? I've come to help you.'

The youngster opened his eyes and said something in a language Aemon didn't understand. Then with a cry, he pulled his hand away and tried to crawl off into the undergrowth.

Perhaps he belonged to Josephus' party. He'd try him in Latin.

'I am a friend,' Aemon said.

The boy didn't reply but he ceased struggling. He began to say something in the strange language, then glancing down at his nakedness, closed his eyes and curled up tightly.

Aemon wrapped his tattered cloak around the youth, hoping that the stains didn't show up too badly in the dusk, then putting his good arm behind the boy's shoulders, helped him to stand. The lad clung to Aemon and seemed in danger of falling again, so Aemon put one of the boy's arms around a tree trunk and said. 'Wait. I have a donkey.'

Somehow he got the youngster onto the animal's back and supporting him against the shoulder of his crippled side, clumsily took the bridle in his other hand. The heavy body lolled against him almost knocking him off his feet. He staggered, and pushed the boy upright again. Fortunately, the donkey seemed to understand for it walked slowly, picking its way carefully along the rough track as though to avoid hurting its rider.

The boy's body lurched again and Aemon only just managed to steady him in time to prevent him falling off. He'd never get him to the village at this rate. He could see the light of Mara's fire not far ahead; he'd take him there. If he gave Mara the two coins Josephus had given him that would pay Mara to feed the boy and stay at home to look after him. The new cloak would have to wait a little longer.

Mara ran out on hearing Aemon's call, and with her eldest boy to help her, carried the youth into her little house. She asked Aemon to go with the girl to fetch water from the well and when he returned the boy was propped up in bed talking to Mara in Latin.

Mara's Latin was good; she'd often cooked for the Romans when they came to do business with her husband. She translated for Aemon as she washed the blood from the youngster's head.

'He's from one of the Roman provinces – I don't recognise the name – but he's here with his uncle buying lead. The rest of the party's some miles behind and he'd gone back with a message. The thieves took everything; his horse, his money belt, even his clothes. They must have thought he was dead for when he came round he'd been pushed under a bush at the edge of the track where nobody would find him.'

'Ask him if he's with Josephus. If he is I'll go and tell his uncle he's here.'

Mara spoke a few words to the youth.

'He says there's no need. They aren't expecting him back till tomorrow.'

She patted Aemon's good arm anxiously. 'You should go home before dark. The thieves might still be about. If you call round in the morning I'll get him to write a note to his uncle – he says he can read and write. Then maybe you can go and get some suitable clothes for him.'

The youth propped himself painfully up on his elbow and beckoned to Aemon to come to him. He said something in a language Aemon didn't understand, then gently touched the scarred face and withered arm before falling back upon the bed exhausted.

It was dark when Aemon finally reached the village; the torches at his uncle's gate casting great shadows across the courtyard. Two of his cousins looked out to see who was approaching.

'Oh it's only Aemon,' said the elder dismissively.

'And I suppose you'll be wanting to be fed.' His aunt's voice came loudly from within the kitchen. She emerged, wearing her usual cross expression.

Suddenly she screamed.

'Witchcraft!' She yelped, pointing at Eamon with the ladle she was carrying. 'Look at him. His bad eye's come back to life and it's staring at me!' Then hastily making a sign against evil, she rushed back indoors.

His uncle emerged, followed closely by his sons.

'Oh witchcraft is it? We'll soon see about that, won't we lads.' Then lifting his cudgel he lunged towards Aemon.

Aemon grabbed at his uncle's hand and slowly bent back his arm until the cudgel dropped, hitting the packed earth of the courtyard with a thud. His uncle stood helpless, with mouth open and eyes staring.

The other two rushed at him then stopped too.

'He used his withered arm,' one of them said shakily, then they all rushed back to the house, slamming the door behind them. Aemon could hear the heavy bolts being dragged across inside. There would be no shelter for him there tonight.

He gazed about him bewildered, not knowing what to do, then he remembered what his cousin had said. He looked at his injured arm: it hung straight and true beside him. He held both hands out in front of him and wriggled his fingers. Both hands seemed to be normal. Then he raised his arms above his head and turned them from side to side. His withered arm was healed.

Scarcely able to believe the wondrous thing that had happened to him, he looked about him for something in which to see his face, but could find nothing. Pans, basins, everything of polished metal had been taken indoors for the night.

Then he laughed. He didn't need to see his face. He could feel the skin, smooth and unlined beneath his hand. He shut his good eye and found he could still see the huts silhouetted against the sky. His bad eye must have returned to normal too!

He turned and picked up the donkey's halter. With two strong arms he could earn a living. He would carry loads, help in the fields – maybe even work his own mine as his father had done. He could go and live with Mara now. He'd help her nurse the foreign boy then take him back to his people. Whoever he was Aemon knew he was good. He didn't know how he'd healed him but he had; there was no other explanation for it.

Aemon could see the glow of Mara's fire in the distance, and the mist rising from the marshes diffused the light into a halo around the little hut. It seemed to shimmer with a hope for the future, and as he walked towards the light, he knew that nothing in this world would ever be the same again.